LOYAL TO THE SOIL

Lock Down Publications and Ca$h
Presents
Loyal to the Soil
A Novel by *Jibril Williams*

Lock Down Publications

P.O. Box 944
Stockbridge, Ga 30281
www.lockdownpublications.com

This is a work of fiction. Names, characters, places, and incidents either are products of the author's imagination or are used fictitiously. Any similarity to actual events or locales or persons, living or dead, is entirely coincidental.

Lock Down Publications
Like our page on Facebook: Lock Down Publications @
www.facebook.com/lockdownpublications.ldp

Book interior design by: **Shawn Walker**
Edited by: **Kiera Northington**

Stay Connected with Us!

Text **LOCKDOWN** to 22828 to stay up-to-date with new releases, sneak peaks, contests and more...

Thank you!

Submission Guideline.

Submit the first three chapters of your completed manuscript to ldpsubmissions@gmail.com, subject line: Your book's title. The manuscript must be in a .doc file and sent as an attachment. Document should be in Times New Roman, double spaced and in size 12 font. Also, provide your synopsis and full contact information. If sending multiple submissions, they must each be in a separate email.

Have a story but no way to send it electronically? You can still submit to LDP/Ca$h Presents. Send in the first three chapters, written or typed, of your completed manuscript to:

LDP: Submissions Dept
P.O. Box 944
Stockbridge, Ga 30281

DO NOT send original manuscript. Must be a duplicate.

Provide your synopsis and a cover letter containing your full contact information.

Thanks for considering LDP and Ca$h Presents.

Jibril Williams

CHAPTER 1

COLEMAN FEDERAL PRISON...

Malaya entered the visitation room promptly at 7:50 am. All eyes were on her as she entered the room. She locked eyes with her two closest Muslim sisters, Keisha and Anya. They squealed like schoolgirls at the sight of each other. Keisha, Anya and Malaya hugged each other tightly in a bear hug. You would have thought it had been ages since they had seen each other, but they were just at the Masjid together yesterday for Jumah, the Islamic sermon. Malaya kissed each of her sisters on both cheeks. They quickly took their seats and waited for their names to be called for visitation processing.

The relationship between Malaya, Anya, and Keisha was a problematic one to explain. Malaya was the glue that held the trio together. Truth be told, Anya and Keisha harbored a deep dislike for each other, though no one would know it just by looking at them.

Keisha was a difficult individual to describe. No one could deny anything about her could be considered "natural beauty," as there wasn't a damn thing natural about her. From her flowing weave to false lashes and nails, mostly everything about Keisha was bought at the local beauty supply.

She had a walk that demanded everyone's attention when she entered a room. Many men said there was just something so mesmerizing about her, and women scoffed it must be the voluptuous ass and the miniature waist that attracted so many.

Keisha was what we call a "born Muslim," meaning she came from a long line of Muslims. Both of her parents were Muslim, her grandparents, and even her great grandparents were Muslim. Stories have been told that her great-grandparents were close confidants of Malcolm X. With her family being so rooted in Islam, one would expect Keisha to be stronger in her faith. The truth is, Keisha wore Islam more like a designer outfit, some days she sported it, and some days she didn't. Today was one of those days she didn't.

Keisha's husband, Abdul Hakeem, affectionately known as Dinkles, had been in love with Keisha since high school. The day after they graduated high school together, Dinkles mustered up the nerve to ask Keisha's dad for permission to marry her. Overjoyed she was marrying a man of the same faith, Keisha's father quickly obliged. Her father believed with a strong Muslim man to guide her, Keisha would live a more righteous and virtuous life. Well, sometimes all parents can do is hope and pray for the best.

Dinkles knew he was in over his head by marrying Keisha. Dinkles came from a hard-working, blue-collar family, whereas Keisha was born with a silver spoon in her mouth. Keisha grew up with nannies and housekeepers. Dinkles knew by marrying Keisha, he not only married his first love, but he also married into a lifestyle he knew very little about. Dinkles promised to give Keisha the life she was always accustomed to, and he did.

Unfortunately, the only way Dinkles knew how to do that was to sell drugs. At first, he had to rely on the expertise of his drug dealing cousins. Though he was fairly new to the hustler life, he was actually pretty good at it. Keisha and Dinkles loved the high life longer than most hustlers. All good things must come to an end, and they certainly did. Dinkles got busted and luckily for him, the detectives made mistake after mistake during his arrest and confiscation of the "evidence." At first, Dinkles was looking at two life sentences, but after his high-priced attorney dragged the prosecution through the mud, he ended up only getting five to fifteen years.

Now for Anya...

Anya was the friend every woman needed, or at least hoped, to have. She was loyal and trustworthy. She was always honest and told you the truth, no matter how much you may not have wanted to hear it. Anya and Malaya shared a special bond because they both discovered Islam through their incarcerated husbands, and they took their Shahadas (testimony of Islamic faith) together also. They shared an unbreakable Islamic bond, and no matter what, would always be sisters to the end.

Loyal to the Soil

Anya's husband's name is Muhammad. Muhammad would be home in twelve years, and though that should be something for Anya to celebrate, she was in utter turmoil. There was nothing Anya wouldn't do for Muhammad. Truth be told, there wasn't anything she hadn't done for him. Anya depleted all their money and assets on attorneys and court fees. It wasn't all in vain. Because she was able to afford that high priced attorney.

What Muhammad didn't know was that the bank had started to foreclose on their home. Last week, the finance company came to repossess their Lexus and Audi. Now Anya had to resort to driving her old Chevy Malibu. Anya was one of those women who always seemed to have the uncanny ability to remain calm in the face of a storm, but the worry was starting to cause her to slowly unravel.

To add insult to injury, Anya's daughter, A'idah, was battling acute lymphocytic leukemia, otherwise known as ALL. Unlike other forms of leukemia, ALL progresses rapidly. With no insurance and funds dwindling away, Anya had to stand by and watch life slowly being drawn out of A'idah's frail six-year-old body.

Jibril Williams

CHAPTER 2

SECRET UNTOLD

Eighteen months ago...

A'idah was a radiant four-year-old girl, with the most beautiful sun-kissed complexion. When she looked at you, you were instantly mesmerized by those golden eyes. Her eyes matched the natural highlights in her hair. A'idah was weak and pale. She constantly whined to Anya, "Ummi, (meaning Mommy) my bones hurt!" Fearing the worst, Anya tried to comfort her only child.

Next came the non-stop nosebleed, along with so much bleeding from her gums, Anya could no longer deny the fact something was seriously wrong. Anya took A'idah to the pediatrician. After countless tests, the doctor confirmed Anya's worst fear, A'idah had leukemia.

Anya didn't know how to tell Muhammad their only daughter was fighting a disease that could possibly take her life. Anya feared that if she talked about the disease, it would bring life to the truth she refused to face.

When Muhammad was sentenced to prison, Anya thought she was going to die. If it wasn't for A'idah, and her strong belief in Islam and the afterlife, she certainly would have killed herself. Six months after Muhammad went to prison, Anya still had not come to terms with the fact that she would have to raise A'idah alone. Losing Muhammad almost killed her, and Anya was certain losing A'idah would definitely kill her.

Anya decided it was best not to tell Muhammad just yet about A'idah. She needed to get a second opinion. *Doctors could be wrong, and there was no sense in worrying Muhammad, when he was already going through so much in prison.* Besides, Muhammad was in the hole again. This was the third time in the last year, and each time, the prison officials couldn't make any of their false allegations stick. The system was designed to break men like Muhammad, by any means necessary.

He had endured countless shakedowns or cell searches, harassment and scrutiny, from the rookies to the warden himself. Muhammad had been strip searched in public, thrown in a dry cell and not given a bath for twelve days, but yet his spirit was not broken. He had been demeaned beyond belief. Through all of this, he remained strong. Anya couldn't imagine what the news about A'idah would do to him. This might just be what would send him over the edge.

CHAPTER 3

RECONNECTED

Anya glanced over at Malaya, wondering who would be called next to be processed for visitation. Anya was the first to get called and Malaya got called next. No one was surprised when they skipped over Keisha to process Malaya. Keisha had been getting harassed by the prison guards for the last six months. She had grown pretty much accustomed to it. Every so often, she got fed up and cussed someone out.

The guards convinced themselves that Keisha was smuggling drugs, but Keisha just blamed it on jailhouse snitches. Those jailhouse snitches always placed the blame on someone else to take the heat off of themselves. That is just how prison politics worked. Every few months they would drop a dime on someone else, and the vicious cycle would continue.

Malaya anxiously sat in the hard, plastic chairs in the visiting room, just contemplating what she would say to Velli. It seemed like an eternity since they had last spoken. She didn't know how he would react to seeing her. Should she just wrap her arms around his neck, or should she let him make the first move? The anticipation of seeing him was overwhelming. Her palms were sweaty, and she squirmed in her seat like a little girl on her first day of school.

The door opened and Velli emerged. Malaya couldn't read the expression on his face. It seemed like it took an eternity for him to make it over to Malaya. Just seeing her wearing his favorite color and looking so beautiful, he couldn't resist the urge to wrap his arm around her. Velli scooped Malaya up as she wrapped her arms around his neck. Months of pain and pent-up frustration were instantly released.

Malaya came there with the intention of giving Velli a piece of her mind, but now she stood there crying like a punk. Velli always knew exactly what Malaya needed and when she needed it. He held her tightly and gently wiped the tears from her face, while kissing her forehead. Ashamed, Malaya lowered her face. Gently, Velli

cupped Malaya's face in his hands and guided her lips towards his. They kissed like they were the only two people in the room. Time stood still when Velli kissed her. She melted into him and the two instantly became one. As they parted, Malaya could not even remember why she was mad at him in the first place.

They sat down and sighed in relief. Neither one of them could deny their connection. Their love was magnetic and mesmerizing. Velli decided to speak first. "Malaya, you know I have always loved you. I loved you from the first moment we met. Even before you knew you loved me, I loved you, but I can no longer stand by and watch you go through this anymore. I feel so helpless and as a man, I can no longer allow myself to feel this way anymore—"

"But—" Malaya interrupted.

"No, please hear me out. I cannot stand to hear you cry out for me on the phone, when I cannot hold and comfort you. It tortures me, Malaya. I have such a beautiful wife and I cannot hold, cannot touch, cannot make love to, cannot take care of and it is so damn frustrating. Sometimes I feel like I am holding you back. Your life's on hold while I am here. I feel like I have let you down. Everything was riding on me getting a new trial, and now that possibility is lost. I cannot stand the thought of losing you, so I would rather let you go before I do."

"Velli, when I married you, I knew exactly who I was marrying and what I was marrying into. The only thing you ever promised was to love me forever. I am only expecting you to do exactly what you promise, or our vows were in vain.

Well, how do you know I don't already have what I deserve? Most importantly, I have what I want. I want my husband. I need my husband. Stop shutting me out. I told you I would always be here, and I meant that. So, we lost our first battle, but the war has just begun. It is time for us to strategize. It is time for us to fight." Malaya strained to fight back her tears.

"You may have a different opinion when you hear what else I have to say. I cannot just sit back and wait for shit to happen. I gotta make shit happen. I need to do what I gotta do to generate some funds here. I know how you worry, and I know how you feel about

that, but the type of lawyer I need costs money—money we do not have right now."

Malaya's heart took a few shallow beats as her chest began to tighten. Just the thought of what Velli was saying almost brought her to tears again. She had always been the type of person to abide by the law and always do what was right, but now Velli was telling her he wanted to resort to the lifestyle that landed him in prison in the first place. Malaya was speechless.

"You don't have anything to say?" Velli inquired.

"Well, what can I say? It seems like you have already made your decision without even considering what I think."

"How can you say I didn't consider what you think? I knew this would be your reaction, but it is time for me to start to make a way out of no way. I have to step up, Malaya, and I don't expect you to support me, but I would hope that you would understand."

Malaya could see the determined look in Velli's eyes, and she could feel the sense of pain and desperation emanating from his soul. How could she not understand what he must be going through? This was her husband, and she must support him, but she didn't have to like what he did. Velli's decision had been made. Malaya and Velli sat in silence for what seemed like a lifetime.

Velli was in shock and overcome by emotion when Malaya spoke. "I know you feel like I worry too much, but it is only because I love you. If anything was to ever happen to you in here, and I couldn't get to you, it would kill me. I trust you know what you're doing and why you're doing it, and that is enough for me. No matter what may happen, I will always be here for you."

A smirk crossed Velli's face. "How did I ever get so lucky to have you? You always amaze me." While the guards were not looking, Velli sneaked a quick kiss and ran his hands up between her thighs.

Jibril Williams

CHAPTER 4

DESPERATION

Anya and Malaya both pulled up at Keisha's house, at the same time, for their weekly get together. Typically, they'd start their day by having brunch and studying the Quran, but here lately Keisha had not been "feeling it." She had been in a strange mood. When they exited their cars, they were confronted by Drake's song, "Started From the Bottom" booming from Keisha's house, and they both knew that Keisha was in one of her moods again.

Anya and Malaya greeted each other with, "As Salaam Alaikum," and a puzzled look on their faces. Apparently, Keisha had company. It was Anya's initial reaction to start walking towards her car. She was not in any mood for Keisha's mess today, but Keisha swung the door open before Anya had a chance to make it to her car.

"Salaams, my sisters!" Keisha shouted exuberantly.

Malaya and Anya exchanged confused looks and proceeded into Keisha's house. They were nearly knocked down with the overwhelming smell of weed and the sound of men's voices radiating from the living room. Anya stopped dead in her tracks, and immediately turned on her heels, heading back towards her car.

"Malaya, just let yourself back in when you finish with Anya," Keisha said with a smirk. She knew exactly what to do to get Anya to leave.

"Malaya, you know I love you like a sister, but Keisha is not on her deen (belief and practice of Islam) right now. I got too much going on right now to be subjected to her foolishness. Why would she invite us over here when she has company sitting in there getting high? I know that is your girl, but you know she ain't right!" Anya exclaimed.

"I know, but we need her help if we want to launch our business," Malaya pleaded.

Anya and Malaya had plans to start an Internet business, selling gift baskets. They needed Keisha's expertise as a web designer to launch their business.

"I know we need her, but the problem is Keisha doesn't need anyone. People like her are only out for themselves, no matter what the cost. I tolerate Keisha because of you. Quite frankly, she is traveling a road I don't ever want to go down. Malaya, I just cannot deal with her today. I was looking forward to spending the day with my sister, praising Allah and coming up with a best friend, but she knew something was wrong." Sensing Anya's disgust, Malaya decided not to press the issue and just let Anya go home.

"Okay, girl. I will just stay here for a while to see if I can get something accomplished with Keisha, and then I am heading home too. I will call you when I get home."

"I see this was a little too much for your girl, huh? She needs to recognize Shaytan (Satan) is everywhere and merely avoiding him doesn't make him go away," Keisha scoffed.

"Yeah, well I don't recommend inviting Shaytan into your home either, Keisha. What is wrong with you? You knew we were coming over, so why would you have them over here? You know Anya doesn't know anything about all this, or your secret endeavors. Have you lost your damn mind? I don't know what the hell you have been smokin', but you really have gone crazy! You know she is going to tell Muhammad, and he will tell Dinkles. Yeah, you remember Dinkles—your husband, right?" Malaya was furious.

"Okay, Malaya, now you have crossed the damn line! You know I love Dinkles! But love doesn't pay the damn bills around here."

"Oh really? Is this how you show him you love him, by having some nigga layin' up in the house he paid for? Is this how you display loyalty to your husband? Now, what you do in the street is your business, but when you bring that mess into the home you share with your husband? That is downright dirty and you know it, Keisha!"

Malaya was in shock as she glanced into the living room to see three niggas sprawled out on Dinkles' couch with blunts hanging

out of their mouths. Knowing Keisha, that scene came as no surprise to Malaya, but what was shocking was all the money she saw on the coffee table. There was more money than Malaya had ever seen at one time. Suddenly, she was at a loss for words.

"Well, at least now I see I have your undivided attention. It is amazing what money does to broke niggas," Keisha mumbled under her breath.

"What the fuck did you just say?" Malaya was suddenly snapped back into reality.

"My bad, girl. This weed got me trippin. Listen, what I needed to talk to you about, didn't concern Anya anyway. I know you two want to start an Internet business making gift baskets or some shit, but are you trying to make money or just chump change?"

"You know the kind of money I need to hire a lawyer to get my husband out of jail, so don't patronize me with bullshit ass questions!" Malaya shouted.

"Actually, you need to stop patronizing your own pockets and learn how to make some real money."

Malaya heard those three niggas snickering in the background and was instantly infuriated. She stormed past Keisha into the living room and stopped dead in her tracks when she was confronted with a familiar face.

"Mikey?" Malaya couldn't believe who she was seeing. Mikey stood up and prepared to embrace Malaya, just as she turned to Keisha.

"This is the 'Mike' you have been telling me about?" Malaya inquired.

Instantly jealous and suspicious, Keisha responded with, "Yeah, and how da hell do you know him?"

Malaya smiled. No matter how beautiful Keisha knew she was, she was still the most insecure woman Malaya had ever met.

Mike was confused by Malaya's reaction to seeing him. He decided just to lay low to see how the whole situation played out.

Though Keisha wasn't really convinced of Malaya's answer, she decided to let it go for now.

"Well, Mikey and I have a proposition for you," announced Keisha with her newfound confidence. "We want to show you how to make some real money."

"Yeah, well something tells me I am not going like what I am going to hear, but I am listening, Keisha. Go ahead. What is your proposition?"

Mike took his cue to step in. "Well, you obviously know who I am and what I do. I am sure you also heard about the recent bust that has several of my right-hand men in jail."

"Yeah, I saw it on the news." Malaya tried to appear disinterested in what Mike had to say.

"To make a long story short, I need a runner."

Malaya couldn't believe her ears. "Awww, hell no! Why the hell are you telling me? I would think a man of your caliber would have no trouble getting someone to drive your drugs from Texas for you. What's wrong, you don't still have the police department on our payroll anymore?"

Keisha quizzically raised an eyebrow, trying to understand how Malaya knew where Mike got his drugs from and who he employed. She remained quiet and continued to take it all in.

Malaya realized she was running her mouth a little too much and tried to clean it up by saying, "I am not dumb, and I am not as green as most people may think. I watch the news and I know most narcotics come out of Texas, and all kingpins have the police on payroll."

"Well, actually, everything that you say is correct, but I am having some trouble with this new police chief. He is trying to crack down on the drug trade. Right now, he is untouchable. It will only be a matter of time and he will be working for me too," Mike boasted.

He is still as cocky as ever, Malaya thought. "As nice as all of that sounds, that still doesn't explain what this has to do with me."

Keisha suddenly got tired of the back-and-forth charade between Mike and Malaya and decided to take over the conversation. "Listen, you wonder how I have managed to maintain my lifestyle right? Well, this is how I do it. All I have to do is fly to Texas, pick

up the rental, and drive the product back. Simple. It is the quickest five thousand I've ever made. The more trips you take, the more money you make. It's nothing for me to make thirty thousand in a month."

Malaya just stood there in shock, staring at Keisha and wondered how long Keisha had been doing this. All this time Malaya thought Keisha was living off of some secret stash of money Dinkles had put away, when all along she had been a drug runner. *Well, that explains why she would disappear for a day or two at a time.* Malaya wondered if Dinkles knew anything about this. Malaya thought, *if I could make six trips, that would be the money needed to put down on the retainer for Velli's lawyer.* Malaya quickly snapped out of it. She wouldn't even consider the thought, no matter how tempting it sounded. She was a schoolteacher and more importantly, she was Muslim. Unlike Keisha, that actually meant something to her. Besides, how would Velli react to her running drugs?

This explained all the changes Keisha had been going through. She was not the same person. Some might say she wasn't the best Muslim, but at least she used to have a heart. She was stomping on Dinkles's heart, and Malaya doubted she even cared. Malaya just stared at Keisha as tears began to well up in her eyes. She was losing her friend to the streets. Once a man like Mikey got ahold of you, there was no turning back. Malaya looked at Keisha one more time, before pitifully shaking her head and walking out the front door.

Jibril Williams

CHAPTER 5

SECRET REVEALED

The day after...

"As Salaamu Alaikum, sis," Anya solemnly greeted Malaya.

"Wa Alaikum As Salaam, ir Rahman tu Allah wa Barakatuh. Before we even start talking about Keisha and her madness, I just want you to know I do not think you were wrong for leaving. Actually, I wish I would have left with you," Malaya replied.

"I wish you would have too, but that's not why I am calling."

Malaya could sense something was wrong with Anya. "What's up, girl? Are you mad at me for staying? Look, I left shortly after you did. I just had to let Keisha know she is wrong for how she treated you."

"Listen, I can't talk for long. My cell is about to go dead. Can you meet me at Mercy General?"

"Mercy Gen-wait! Anya, are you sick?" The line went dead.

Panic set in. Anya had sickle-cell anemia, and usually when she had an "episode," she called Malaya. Malaya was puzzled, and she couldn't seem to function or comprehend why Anya wouldn't have called her sooner. What could be wrong with Anya, and why didn't she call Malaya and have her take her to the hospital? Malaya threw on a pair of sweats, her hijab (head covering) and she was out the door.

At Mercy General

Malaya rushed up to the emergency room nurse's station. "Yes, I need to see what room Anya Muhammad is in."

"The pedia-what? Oh no, something happened to A'idah!" Malaya ran towards the stairs. There was no time to wait for the elevator. As she raced up the flight of steps, she doubled over in pain as

though someone had punched her in the stomach. Something was terribly wrong.

The closer Malaya got to the room, the more the pain increased. By the time she made it to room 212, she was in agonizing pain. Before entering the room, Malaya said a silent little prayer. *Ya Allah! Please let A'idah be all right, Ameen.*

Malaya gently pushed the door open to see an enormous, white hospital bed covered in so many tubes, it was nearly impossible to see the tiny figure in the bed. At the sound of the door opening, her eyes fluttered open. Those golden eyes were unmistakable. Her eyes were unfocused and glued to Malaya. It took a minute for A'idah to realize who was at her door.

"Auntie Lay-Lay?" A'idah was so weak, Malaya barely heard her.

"Yes, my golden girl. How are you feeling? Where's Ummi?" asked Malaya.

"Went to get ice. My throat's dry." A'idah closed her eyes.

Malaya couldn't understand what was going on there. She had never seen A'idah look like this. A'idah was rarely ever sick.

It was killing Malaya to see A'idah's face so ashen and her body so motionless. Determined to get some answers, Malaya turned to storm out of the room and find the nurse's station, but she ran into Anya. With one look, Anya could see the fury in Malaya's eyes, and she knew in a matter of minutes, Malaya was going to snap. Anya grabbed Malaya by the crook of her arm and quickly ushered her out of the room and into a nearby stairwell.

Anya hoped to be able to speak first, but Malaya dug into her as soon as they entered the stairwell.

"Before I allow myself to get upset, I am going to give you the opportunity to tell me what is going on," Malaya growled through clenched teeth.

"Listen, Malaya. I have spent many sleepless nights trying to think of how I am going to tell you this, and I don't know any way to tell this but just to say it... A'idah has been diagnosed with leukemia."

Malaya felt like someone had their hands around her throat, squeezing the life out of her. She doubled over with her hands on her knees, gasping for air. Suddenly consumed with anger, she lunged at Anya. Anya grabbed Malaya by the wrists and they both fell to the floor, in a ball of shrieking cries. Malaya wanted to be angry at Anya for not telling her sooner and for allowing herself to have to go through this alone. They both were in a heap on the floor crying uncontrollably. Anya finally let out the tears she had wanted to let go of, and Malaya cried for Anya and for A'idah.

After what seemed like an eternity, neither of them could cry anymore. They were exhausted and their eyes were nearly swollen shut. Without any words spoken between them, they both stood and walked solemnly back to A'idah's room. She appeared to be sleeping, though it seemed to be a restless sleep. Malaya watched closely as A'idah's chest rose and fell with tremendous effort.

The nurse entered the room and explained she had taken the liberty to bring in a rollaway bed for them to spend the evening with A'idah. "I am so glad to finally see someone give Ms. Anya a break. Every time little A'idah has a setback, Ms. Anya sleeps here day in and day out." Sensing the tension, the nurse exited the room as quickly as she entered.

Malaya thought, *every time A'idah has a setback? Now just how long has this been going on? Obviously, Muhammad doesn't know because he would have told Velli, and Velli would have told me.* Just as Malaya's anger was getting ready to consume her logic, A'idah opened her eyes and smiled weakly at Malaya.

"Auntie Lay-Lay, will you stay with me tonight?"

Malaya thought, *if your momma wasn't so damned secretive, I could have been spending the night here a long time ago.* Malaya didn't want to make a bad situation worse, so she bit her tongue, and did not give the slightest indication that she was upset.

"Of course, A'idah, I will stay here tonight, only if Ummi promises to go home and get some rest."

Anya couldn't deny A'idah for much longer. She had been asking for Malaya for a while now, and it was time for Malaya to know the truth and spend some alone time with A'idah. Anya felt horrible

for not telling her best friend, and now she realized that was probably the wrong choice. Now she was forced to wonder how Muhammad would handle the tragic news, and would her friendship with Malaya ever be the same?

Anya and Malaya locked eyes for a brief moment before Anya walked over and kissed A'idah on the forehead. Before exiting the room, Anya whispered in Malaya's ear, "Please let me be the first person to tell my husband."

CHAPTER 6

THE FIRST OF MANY LIES

Spring Break...

Ever since Anya told Malaya about A'idah, they had been alternating their nights in the hospital. A'idah was released from the hospital after nine long days. According to A'idah's doctors, her hospital stays were increasing in frequency and duration. The doctors said that was the progression of the disease and it was to be expected. A'idah would have good days and bad days. Malaya was determined to make sure her good days outweigh her bad.

"As Salaam Alaikum," Malaya cheerfully greeted a caller on her phone.

"What's up, girl?" At first Malaya was taken aback by the harshness of Keisha's voice and by the fact that she did not return the greeting.

"Since when did you start not returning the Most High's greeting?" Malaya inquired.

"Since when do you start slapping the hand that feeds you?" Keisha retorted.

"What the—" was Malaya's initial reaction to cuss Keisha out. What the hell did Keisha mean by, "Slapping the hand that feeds me?"

"Look, Keisha, I know you may have helped me out from time to time, but you are hardly the hand that feeds me, so let's not get it twisted. I have helped you out just as much as you have helped me."

"Who said it was my hand I was referring to?" Then panic set in. What has Mikey told Keisha? Keisha covered the phone, having a muffled conversation with someone in the background.

Malaya's palms began to sweat, trying to figure out what Keisha knew about Mikey.

Keisha came back to the phone. "My bad, girl. I was smokin'. You know how that shit has me trippin'. Open the door, I am pullin' up in your driveway now."

Damn! Malaya was emotionally drained, dealing with the situation with A'idah and was in no mood to deal with Keisha.

Keisha strolled in looking like she just stepped off of a runway, sporting Michael Kors from head to toe.

"Girl, you look like shit!" Leave it to Keisha to tell you the heartfelt truth.

"Well, thanks and you look fabulous, as usual," Malaya replied.

"And you could too, but you are letting your goods go to waste. I am getting ready to show you how to use what you got to get what you want. Pack a bag. Our flight leaves in four and a half hours."

"What the hell? I told you, I am not running any drugs! What you do with, or for that nigga Mike, is your business, but keep me out of it!"

Keisha knew it was going to be hell to get Malaya to take this trip with her. She recognized it was time for her to act like a concerned friend. "Look, girl, I know you really need to start saving some major funds in order to help with Velli's legal fees," Keisha replied. "I convinced Mike to pay you the five thousand just to fly out to Texas with me and all you gotta do is follow me back to Tampa from Texas, after I meet with the connect."

Malaya could not help herself. Being as green as she was, she thought that was a sweet deal. "So, you're telling me that all I have to do is fly out to Texas with you, then follow you back to Tampa in a rental car, and I get five grand?" Malaya said.

"That's all you have to do, girl. You're my sister. You know I'm going to look out for you," Keisha replied with a conniving smirk on her face.

"How long will we be gone?" Malaya asked.

"No more than three days." When Keisha noticed Malaya used the word "we," she knew she had Malaya right where she wanted her.

Malaya knew she'd have to tell Anya something to explain why she was out of town, but her real dilemma was lying to Velli, something she'd never done before. "Oh Allah, forgive me," Malaya mumbled.

Keisha was getting impatient. "Girl, are you down or what?" she asked Malaya with her face contorted.

"Yeah, Keisha, I'm going. I need that money, but you cannot say shit to Anya. If this shit gets back to Velli, he will go crazy," Malaya pleaded.

Keisha rolled her eyes at Malaya's request. "Look, it's two pm. Now, the plane leaves at six-thirty. I'll pick you up at four, so we can grab a bite to eat before the plane takes off. Plus, I got your Mikey waiting for me in the car," Keisha said with a smile on her face. Hearing that comment forced Malaya to get on the defensive.

"What do you mean, *my* Mikey?" Malaya asked, stepping to Keisha.

"Girl, I'm just playing!" Keisha said, stepping back from Malaya. "Just make sure you are ready by four!" Keisha yelled while heading towards the door.

Malaya called out to Keisha, "Thanks, girl! I owe you one!"

"That's what sisters are for," Keisha stated as she walked out the door,

Soon, Malaya would be heading to the airport with Keisha, getting ready to embark upon an event that would forever change her life.

Jibril Williams

CHAPTER 7

UNVEILED

At 4:00 pm sharp, Keisha was there to pick Malaya up, blowing the horn like she was crazy. Malaya walked out the house without her Islamic garments or head covering on, feeling naked without them, but no one could deny the fact that she looked so sexy in her pink Prada sweatsuit. I haven't seen you in plain clothes in years!" Keisha said with excitement, "But what's the real reason for you abandoning your hijab?"

"I just don't want to get harassed by the TSA agents," replied Malaya. "You know how they are. They see you with a hijab or kufi on your head and they swear you're gonna pull another nine-eleven, and I don't have time for that shit today! Not to mention, you would look odd standing next to me!"

Keisha burst out laughing, "Girl, you are on a trip, but it's the truth," checking her rearview mirror. "I see why Velli wants to keep you covered up twenty-four-seven. You got a bangin' body," Keisha said while eyeing Malaya's shapely thighs and round ass.

"I do not cover up twenty-four-seven for Velli. I do it because Allah commands all the believing women to do so," Malaya retorted.

Malaya was five-one, with the most flawless caramel, sunkissed complexion. Nestled about her high Indian cheekbones, were the most captivating almond brown eyes any man has ever looked into. Her picture-perfect smile could light up the darkest room with the slightest effort, and that was one of the reasons Velli fell for Malaya. Her jet-black hair, which was usually hidden by a hijab, cascaded in deep waves down to the middle of her back. Her plump, round ass was nothing to play with either. She could attract the attention from all calibers of men, black and white, and even a few women. When Malaya wore her Islamic garments, people often thought she was from Yemen. Malaya was truly in a class of her own.

After Malaya and Keisha grabbed a quick bite to eat from KFC, they headed to Tampa International Airport to catch their flight to Dallas, Texas. Malaya started to panic once she got to the airport.

Damn, I'm really going to go through with this shit. "I can do this," Malaya mumbled, "this is for my husband," reasoning with herself.

They passed through security with no problems. While heading towards the terminal to board their plane, Malaya's stomach started to do flips, and her forehead and hands began to sweat. Keisha noticed this, stopped and turned to Malaya, placed her hands on Malaya's shoulders, and whispered, "Baby girl, you can do this. Just relax," staring into Malaya's eyes. "You're not in harm's way." Keisha reassured Malaya.

Feeling a little better, Malaya smiled and said, "Let's get this money!"

CHAPTER 8

TEXAS IN A TRICK BAG

4 Hours Later...

Keisha and Malaya landed in Dallas, Texas. "Damn, it's hot out here," Keisha said, throwing on her Chanel sunglasses.

"You ain't never lied about that, girl," Malaya agreed with Keisha, pulling her sweat suit jacket off and tying it around her voluptuous ass, protecting her assets from the lustful eyes of men that were checking her out as she walked by.

"We got to pick up the rental cars, then we can swing by the Hilton Inn so I can make some calls," Keisha said. Malaya snatched her cell phone out of her purse to see if she had missed any calls from Velli. Turning her cell off airport mode, she was shocked to see she had not missed a call from her husband. She'd spoken with him that morning and he said he was on his way to the yard to work out with Muhammad.

Malaya received a text from Anya, saying she was on the phone with Muhammad when the institution called for an emergency lockdown. Reading that text, Malaya knew it was going to be a couple of days, or weeks before she heard from Velli. She took that as a sign it was meant for her to get that money. Hertz Rental Car had two, new 2014 Audi's waiting for them there.

Keisha jumped into the candy apple red Audi.

Malaya jumped in the money green Audi and followed Keisha in hot pursuit. Catching up with her at a red light, Malaya flagged Keisha down. "Slow the fuck down! We are here on business," Malaya shouted to Keisha in the next lane. Keisha just gave Malaya the middle finger and pulled off. Next, they arrived at the Hilton Inn, just blocks away from the airport. Keisha jumped out of her Audi while pumping "Diva," Beyonce's song. "A diva is the version of a female hustler." Malaya pulled up behind her, shaking her head and handed her keys to the valet.

Malaya rushed to Keisha with her face twisted all up. "Bitch, what is your problem?" Malaya said, eyeing Keisha.

"What the fuck are you talking about?" Keisha asked Malaya, looking at her sideways.

"I'm talking about that crazy ass driving you were doing in the car. We're here on business and we don't want to attract attention to ourselves," Malaya said with her fist balled up at Keisha.

Keisha snapped. "Who the fuck do you think you are talking to? First off, I'm here on business. You are here just to joy ride. Let's not forget to play our positions, and you stay in your lane."

"Whatever! I just thought since we are sisters, we were in this together," Malaya said.

"Oh, we are in this together," Keisha replied with a cunning look on her face. "Now, let's go get the keys to the rooms so we can settle down and freshen up."

"Let's go. I got to pee, girl," Malaya replied.

Approaching the front desk at the Hilton, the middle-aged desk clerk saw Keisha approaching and turned beet red.

"May I help you?" the desk clerk asked Keisha, as they approached the desk.

"Uh, yes, reservations for Johnson please," Keisha replied, trying to put on her best charm. The clerk typed a few keys on the computer.

"Okay. Here you go," the clerk said, handing Keisha the keys to room 2212. Before releasing the keys to Keisha, the clerk looked Keisha in the eyes and added, "Remember, there's no illegal substance smoking in the rooms."

Snatching the keys from the clerk, Keisha turned and walked away, slinging her round ass from side to side with a vicious attitude.

Finally making it to the room, they both threw their bags on the beds. Malaya headed to the bathroom while Keisha jumped straight on the phone. Malaya examined the bathroom and saw it was laid out with a walk-in shower, with power heads on both sides of the

wall. It had a super big bathtub, enough to seat three people comfortably. She was definitely going to enjoy the tub and shower while she was there.

Getting off the toilet and washing her hands, Malaya exited the bathroom, catching Keisha on the phone with someone she kept calling Mango. Keisha put her hand up, signaling she would be done in a minute. "Yes, Mango, everything is fine. We have no problems," Keisha replied while rolling her eyes. "I'll be there tomorrow morning at eleven am," Keisha confirmed and hung up the phone.

"Who was that?" Malaya asked.

"That was the connect. We have to meet with him tomorrow morning," Keisha replied while eyeing Malaya's thighs and breasts.

Malaya snapped, "What do you mean, *we* have to meet with him tomorrow?" looking at Keisha like she was crazy.

"Girl, calm the fuck down. I have to meet with him tomorrow so he can load the Audi up with the drugs. I need you to follow me tomorrow so we can go shopping while he is doing his thang."

"Oh!" Malaya said, feeling stupid.

"So just chill the fuck out. You act like a corny bitch," Keisha said, getting frustrated with Malaya while dialing Mike's number on her phone

"What does it do?" Mike replied after the second ring.

"Hey, baby!" Keisha cooed seductively into the phone.

"What's good, baby girl? How was the flight?"

"Everything went well, as always," Keisha confirmed.

"That's good. Where is Malaya?"

"She's right here," Keisha said with her lip curled up.

"Put her on the phone," Mike requested.

"For what?" Keisha asked with an attitude.

"Do what I told your ass to do!" Mike shouted into the phone.

Coming into compliance, Keisha handed Malaya the phone. "Your Mikey is on the phone," Keisha said with a sour tone in her voice.

Malaya snatched the phone from Keisha, rolling her eyes. Keisha was starting to get under her skin with this, "Your Mikey" shit.

"Hello," Malaya said into the phone.

"Hey, sweetness!" Mike replied. Just the sound of his voice and him calling her "Sweetness" made her uneasy. "How do you like Texas so far?"

"I haven't seen much of it, since we just got here only an hour ago," Malaya responded. The whole time, Keisha was looking dead into her mouth.

"I told Keisha to give you three thousand for shopping money, and that's not coming out of the five I'm paying you to ride back with Keisha."

"Okay, thanks." Malaya was feeling uncomfortable with the way Keisha was staring at her.

"We have a lot to talk about, Malaya. I'm looking forward to spending some time with you, once you get back to Tampa," Mike said with amusement in his voice.

Not wanting to make Keisha more suspicious than she already was, Malaya just responded with, "Okay," hating herself as soon as the words rolled off her tongue. Feeling satisfied with Malaya's response, Mike told Malaya to give Keisha back the phone.

"Hello," Keisha had an attitude.

"Bitch, what's your fuckin' problem!" Mike barked into the phone.

"Nothing," Keisha replied, putting her attitude into check.

"Make sure you give that shopping money to Malaya."

"Okay," Keisha grumbled with a tight jaw. She ended the phone call and threw the phone on the bed. Keisha turned to Malaya and looked at her for a minute.

"Malaya, let me ask you something."

"Yeah, sure."

"What's the deal with you and Mike?"

"What the fuck you mean, what's the deal with me and Mike?" Malaya got an instant attitude. "There's nothing between Mike and me. Girl, you are trippin'!"

"Yeah, you are right," Keisha said, rubbing her neck. Keisha walked over to her bag lying on the bed and pulled out a fat stack of money. Malaya tried to act like she wasn't shocked by the amount of money on the bed.

"Damn, girl! Where the fuck you get all that money from?" Malaya inquired.

"Where do you think, bitch? From Mike. Here's fifteen hundred for shopping money." Keisha handed Malaya the money. Malaya looked at Keisha funny because she knew Mike told her Keisha was supposed to give her three thousand for shopping, but Malaya didn't want to say anything. She did not want any drama out of Keisha about some punk ass money.

"Thanks, girl," Malaya said, while putting the money in her purse. At that moment, Malaya's phone rang. She looked at the caller ID and it was Anya. "Damn!" Malaya said out loud. She didn't know what to do. She knew she had to answer the call. Telling Keisha to be quiet, Malaya answered the phone. "As Salaamu Alaikum, sister," Malaya mumbled into the phone as though she was sick.

"Wa Alaikum Salaam, sister. What is the matter with you?" Anya was immediately worried.

"I don't know. I think I have a twenty-four-hour bug or something," Malaya lied.

"I was just calling you to check up on you to see if you were going to make it by the house to see A'idah. She's been asking about you."

Feeling bad about not being able to spend time with A'idah broke Malaya's heart. "No, not tonight. I'm really not feeling well, Anya," Malaya continued to lie. "As soon as I feel a little better, I will be over there."

"Okay," Anya replied, "But, where are you? I went by your house an hour ago and you weren't there."

Damn! Malaya thought. "Oh girl, I'm over Keisha's house. She's taking care of me until I get better."

"When did you start hangin' tough with Keisha?" Anya said, feeling a little offended that Malaya hadn't come to her house to let her take care of her.

"I just didn't want to bring what I got around little A'idah."

"Okay, I guess that's a good excuse. You take care and call me if you need anything."

"Okay, I will." Malaya hated lying to her best friend. "Salaamu Alaikum."

"Wa Alaikum As Salaam, sister." Anya hung up.

The next morning, Malaya woke up early to perform her morning prayers. When she finished up, she heard Keisha roll over in bed.

"Are you going to pray this morning?" Malaya asked Keisha.

"No, I'm going to smoke some Kush to get my mind right," Keisha replied, getting out of bed half naked in front of Malaya, wearing a purple lace bra and thong set. Seeing Keisha moving around like that without any shame made Malaya uncomfortable.

Malaya mumbled, "Oh, Allah, forgive her. Surely, she strayed from your path. Forgive us both, because I am about to stray as well."

Keisha sat at the table, smoking her strong scented weed with her legs wide open like a boy, lost in her thoughts. She spoke out loud, "Shit! I need my pussy licked."

Hearing this, Malaya raised her head and looked at Keisha in confusion. "What you say, girl?"

"Nothing, girl. I was just talking to myself."

Malaya, feeling uncomfortable, said she was going to take a long bath. As soon as Malaya closed the bathroom door, Keisha put two fingers in her mouth and placed them in her wet pussy, thinking about what it would be like if Malaya was eating her pussy. "Mmmmmmmm!" Keisha moaned in pure pleasure. The sound of the water filling the tub drowned out Keisha's escapade.

"Girl, are you ready?" Keisha asked Malaya as she walked out of the bathroom a while later.

"Yeah, girl. I'm ready." Malaya's eyes almost popped out of her head when she saw what Keisha had on. "Where the fuck do you think you are going dressed like that?" Malaya asked in disbelief.

"I'm going to see Mango!" Keisha was getting fed up with Malaya's goody-two-shoes bullshit.

"Don't you think you are showing a little too much skin?" Malaya knew Keisha dressed a little risqué, but this was over the top, even for Keisha.

"No, I ain't showing too much!" Keisha said, admiring herself in the mirror.

Keisha wore the shortest skirt she could find, with no panties on, and topped it off with a matching top that revealed her belly button piercing. To add to her sex appeal, she wore her all-black, red bottom heels. Keisha's skirt was so short, you could see the bottom of her voluptuous ass.

"Come on, let's get outta here," Keisha said, heading towards the door.

Malaya followed Keisha while shaking her head, thinking, Keisha *has truly lost all her Islam.*

As Keisha and Malaya were waiting for the car to come around from valet parking, Keisha told Malaya, "When we get to Mango, just smile and be polite."

"Okay, cool," Malaya said without thinking. When both Audis arrived, Keisha jumped in her whip, threw her Burberry shades on, and pulled off into traffic with Malaya right behind her.

Five minutes later, they were pulling up into the huge parking lot of an Audi dealership. Keisha pulled up around back and got out, waiting for Malaya to join her. As soon as Keisha got out of the car, two big Mexican dudes came and took Keisha's car into the service garage.

"Where are they taking the car?" Malaya asked.

"None of your damn business," Keisha said. "The less you know, the better. Now, come on. Let's go meet Mango."

Keisha grabbed Malaya by the hand, walking like only Keisha could, a walk that demanded everybody's attention.

Keisha walked straight to the main office, where Mango was sitting behind his desk, watching the cameras from monitors on the wall.

"Hello, papi," Keisha greeted Mango.

"Hello, mami." Mango was a fat Mexican slob that had major paper, but he kept a low profile by looking dirty, as if he was one of

the people who worked in the service garage. "Good to see you again. Como estas?"

"I'm good," Keisha said, looking Mango in the eyes as he looked at her with lustful eyes and licked his lips. "This is my girl, Malaya, I was telling you about."

Seeing Malaya for the first time, Mango jumped out of his seat and placed a kiss on Malaya's hand. Malaya almost snatched her hand back from Mango. She was not used to men, other than her husband, touching her.

"Hi," Malaya greeted Mango with a half-smile.

"It's a pleasure to meet you, Malaya," Mango replied. Right then, Mango knew immediately Malaya had some class about herself, and there was something special about her. Keisha was becoming too flamboyant and plus, Mango was tired of fucking her. Her pussy got old real quick. He had bigger and better plans for Malaya.

Mango looked at Malaya and said, "Sorry, I don't mean to be rude, but I have some business to discuss with Keisha. Can you please wait out there in the waiting area?" Mango asked.

Welcoming the escape, Malaya quickly exited. As Malaya walked out, Mango checked out how well those jeans were hugging her ass. Mango made up his mind that he had to taste Malaya's pussy before it was all said and done.

Thinking about pussy made Mango's dick stand up. As soon as the door closed behind Malaya, Mango dropped his pants and Keisha didn't hesitate to drop to her knees. She placed his five-inch dick in her mouth and began to suck it nice and slow, just like Mango liked it.

"Yeah, right here," Mango moaned as he placed his hand on the back of Keisha's head. Two minutes later, Mango exploded in Keisha's mouth. Keisha did not miss a beat swallowing every drop. As soon as she was finished, she jumped up and gave Mango a sloppy, wet kiss.

"Mmmmmmm! Thank you, papi," Keisha said with a smile on her face, thinking, this *mothafucka makes me sick*!

Mango dipped in his pocket and pulled out a fat knot of money. "Here you go. Now get the fuck outta here," Mango said as he

handed Keisha the money. "I'll call you when the car is ready for pick up."

"Okay, baby," Keisha said as she was walking out the door.

Keisha and Malaya jumped in the green Audi in route towards downtown Dallas on Highway 35, heading to Grapevine Mills Mall. Keisha ran from store to store, buying all the latest name-brand clothes.

"Why are you not shopping?" Keisha asked Malaya.

"I have better things to spend my money on," Malaya stated, causing Keisha's anger to grow with every word.

"You have to live a little, Malaya. Everything doesn't have to be for Allah and your husband."

"You don't know shit about my husband," Malaya corrected with fire in her eyes.

Keisha knew she had overstepped her boundaries with that comment. "I'm sorry."

"Just don't say shit about my husband." And with that, Malaya walked away with tears in her eyes.

"Where are you going?"

"I'll be waiting for you in the car," Malaya said over her shoulder as a tear slid down her cheek.

On the ride back to the Hilton, Malaya hadn't spoken much to Keisha. They stopped by Pizza Hut and picked up two large pizzas. They also stopped by Mango's to pick up Keisha's car. After taking a long shower, Malaya came out of the bathroom, ate two slices of pizza, and laid down.

Keisha knew Malaya was still bothered by what she said earlier at the mall. She said she was sorry earlier. What else did Malaya want her to say? She needed Malaya focused for the ride back to Florida tomorrow.

"Listen, I am really sorry about what I said earlier."

"It's alright, girl. I'm just tired and I know we have a long drive ahead of us tomorrow," Malaya said with sadness in her voice.

Keisha looked at her watch, and told Malaya, "Look, I'm going to get my kitty scratched. My pussy itch," with a smile on her face.

"What are you talking about now, Keisha?" Malaya questioned.

"I'm talking about going to get me some dick," Keisha replied in her whorish voice, eyeing Malaya. "I need the keys to your car. I can't drive mine because the drugs are in there."

Poor Dinkles, Malaya thought. Not wanting to fuss with Keisha, Malaya handed over the keys to the car. She needed some alone time anyway.

Little did Malaya know Keisha was taking the car back to Mango's Audi dealership so he could load the second car up for another shipment to be taken back to Florida.

The ride back to Florida was a long, but successful trip, though all hell was getting ready to break loose back in Florida...

CHAPTER 9

OTHER SIDE OF THE GAME

Malaya plopped down on the couch exhausted. She had never traveled that far non-stop before. She was glad to be home. Just as she began to doze off, there was a pounding at the front door. Malaya jolted out of her sleep and was instantly irritated. She snatched the door open, ready to cuss out whoever was on the other side of the door.

"Damu?"

"Yeah, sis, are you aight? Where have you been? I been by here for the last couple of days, asking around, and ain't nobody seen you," Damu inquired as he let himself in and laid his cell phone down on the coffee table.

"My bad, Damu. I have been sick for the last couple of days."

"But where were you?" Damu knew Malaya was hiding something.

"I was over at Keisha's. She was taking care of me."

"Well, looking at that bag you got packed over there, you must have moved in with Keisha."

Shit! Malaya forgot she left her overnight bag out.

Sensing Malaya's discomfort, Damu quickly changed the subject. "You know, sis, it is my responsibility to take care of you while Velli is locked up. If something were to happen to you, my brother would kill me!"

"I know, bro. My bad. I will make sure next time to let you know where I am. Thanks for checking on me."

"Aight, sis, lemme get back to work. I got some biz to handle. Call me if you need anything." Damu turned and prepared to walk away.

"Hey, bro! Thanks again for checking on me!" Malaya called after Damu.

Considering all that he had been through, Damu was a really good guy. He had recently moved from Washington, DC. He was heavily into the drug game up there, and then his wife was brutally

murdered. That was all it took to force Damu out of the drug game once and for all. He needed a new lease on life and a fresh start. That was how he ended up in Tampa, Florida, watching over his sister-in-law. Damu lived an honest life now as an owner of a landscaping business.

As Malaya stepped out of the shower, she heard a knock at her door. "Now, who the hell is it?" Malaya grumbled. "I am never going to get some rest! Who is it?"

"It's me, baby girl." Panic instantly set in.

"What the hell is he doing here?" Malaya wondered. "Mike? Listen, this is not a good time."

Mike snickered. "So we still gonna keep playin' this game, huh? How long are we gonna keep pretending, Lay-Lay?"

Lay-Lay. Malaya had not heard him call her that in years. Just hearing it took her on a trip down memory lane, a trip that she knew she had no business visiting.

As Damu was heading down Hillsborough Avenue, he patted his pocket for his cell phone. "Dammit!" Realizing he'd left it over Malaya's, he made a U-turn and headed back towards Malaya's house.

Mike knocked again. "Look, Malaya, you just can't keep avoiding the situation. We will need to talk about it eventually, but that isn't what I'm here about. I am here to pay you."

"I thought I was supposed to meet up with Keisha tomorrow to get paid."

"Well, I wanted to bring it to you myself. Plus, I need to…" Before Mike could finish his sentence, Malaya was swinging the door open, eager to get her money. The quicker she had her hands on that money, the quicker she could start paying for the lawyer Velli needed.

Mike was just standing there with his mouth wide open, eyeing Malay's erect nipples, protruding from the thin fabric of her satin robe. Suddenly aware of her nakedness, Malaya left the door wide open and ran to the bedroom to cover up.

Seizing what Mike believed was the opportunity he had longed for, for quite some time, he followed Malaya towards her bedroom.

He paused outside her bedroom door and watched as she gracefully slid her jeans over her juicy ass. She pulled on a t-shirt and piled her hair on top of her head in a bun. His manhood pressed eagerly against his jeans, hoping for the opportunity to release. Not wanting Malaya to see him lusting after her, Mike quietly returned to the living room.

"Okay. Sorry about that. I had just gotten out of the shower... So, why are you looking at me like that?"

"My bad, Lay-Lay. It has just been so long since we have been alone like that, but here's your money." Mike pulled out a fat stack. "You know this is just the tip of the iceberg. You could go places with me-make more money than you've ever seen. I need a right hand I know will always have my back. Come take a ride with me. I want to show you something."

"Listen, Mikey. We cannot take any trips down memory lane. I am a happily married woman."

"To Velli, right? Didn't he get a life sentence?"

Malaya instantly felt her blood begin to boil. She was hypersensitive when it came to Velli. "Yeah, and?"

"Look, I am not trying to offend you, Lay-Lay. I respect a woman that is down with her man when he's doing time. Keisha told me you are struggling, trying to get the money together to get your man a lawyer, right?"

"Well, for starters, I don't know why Keisha is discussing my business with you, but I am working on getting a lawyer."

"The type of lawyer your man needs takes a limitless cash flow, the type of flow that goes beyond a teacher's salary. Ride with me. Lemme show you what real money looks like."

At first Malaya wanted to get offended, but she shrugged her shoulders, grabbed her purse and keys, and headed out the door. Mike and Malaya pulled up in front of the infamous, Roberts Park Projects. The small-gated community was a world of its own. The drug traffic was crazy. It seemed like the whole city was out there buying coke. The crackheads looked like the walking dead as they walked through the projects, going to get their next high from the young hustlers posted up in the back of the projects.

"Where the hell have you got me at, Mike?" shrieked Malaya.

"This is the hood, baby girl. This is a hustlers' paradise," Mike said with a smile as he opened his car door to get out. Malaysia followed, feeling a little uncomfortable, but she knew she definitely wasn't going to stay in the car by herself. They walked towards the young hustlers at the back of the projects. A light-skinned hustler named Redz hopped off the steps, where all the drug traffic was coming and going, when he saw Mike coming towards him.

"What's up, boss man?" Redz said to Mke.

"Ain't shit. What's good out here?" Mike replied with a no-nonsense tone.

"Just getting this paper, as always."

"That's what's up." Mike was constantly checking out his surroundings.

"Redz, this is Lay-Lay. Lay-Lay, this is my young gun, Redz."

Malaya was thrown off by Mike calling her Lay-Lay in public. "Uh, hi, Redz. How are you?" Malaya said as she shook Redz's right hand, examining the weird-looking tattoo that covered it.

"Nice to meet you, beautiful," Redz replied while eye fucking Malaya and licking his lips. Mike, seeing this, quickly checked Redz.

"Slow down, my nigga, this one right here is already taken."

"My bad, boss man," Redz said, reluctantly releasing Malaya's hand.

Malaya felt like she needed to make things crystal clear to Redz and Mike. "I'm married. Mike and I are just friends."

"Okay, we are friends," Mike said while grabbing Malaya's hand, and leading her across the street to the other side of the projects where the rest of his crew were posted up.

Malaya got this strange feeling as they made their way to apartment 310 on the back hall of the third floor. It was almost like someone was watching their every move.

Mike took out his phone and dialed a number. "I'm outside the door. Open up."

A dark, heavy-set dude stood there, holding an AR-15 assault rifle in his hand. Malaya's heart jumped and started beating a hundred miles a minute, unsure of what was about to unfold.

"Biggz, my nigga. What's poppin'?" Mike addressed the man holding the assault rifle.

"Ain't too much, boss man. Just busting this work down so we can keep that money flowing."

As Malaya stepped fully into the apartment, her mouth fell open. There were eight butt-naked women, standing around a glass topped table, cutting up coke and placing the rocks in small baggies. The women were not even fazed by Mike and Malaya's presence. They kept to their task at hand as if they had a real nine to five job.

"This is the chop shop," Mike said. "Everything coming through here gets broken down to be sold on the streets, or across the street where Redz and his crew is posted up at."

"Why the hell are they naked?" Malaya asked, pointing to the women around the table.

Mike and Biggz burst out laughing. "So those bitches won't steal nothing," Mike replied.

"And this is for the niggaz that be tryna take shit that don't belong to them." Biggz patted the assault rifle he was holding.

"I see you got everything running smoothly in this bitch," Mike said to Biggz. "I'm heading down to the count house," Mike said as he grabbed Malaya's hand and walked out the door.

Mike didn't like staying in the chop shop for long periods of time. He never liked to be boxed in with the work. That was an easy way to get a life sentence. Truth be told, Mike rarely went into the chop shop. The only reason he went to the chop shop today was because he wanted to show Malaya how to get money, and to bring her on his team.

When they exited the chop shop, it seemed the drug traffic had picked up tenfold, and Mike and Malaya had only been in the chop shop for several minutes. Walking three buildings down, they entered into another identical building. Malaya got the same eerie feeling as she did from the building before, like someone was watching them. Mike did as he did before, once he got to apartment 213, he

got on the phone and announced he was at the door. A few moments later, the door opened up and like the chop shop, there was a dude standing there with an assault rifle.

"What it do, Moe B?" Mike asked as they walked in.

"I'm coolin', boss man. Just got that paper counted for you."

"Well, let me get that so I can bounce," Mike said.

"Yo! Bezo, bring that bag!" Moe B called to the back bedroom. A short, bald, brown-skinned dude came out from the back carrying a Louis Vuitton duffle bag.

"What's up, boss man?" greeted the man carrying the bag.

"Ain't too much, Bezo. Just trying to keep my team eating," Mike said as he grabbed the bag from Bezo and headed towards the door.

"That's a hundred and seventy-five thousand. I'll finish counting the rest of the money bag tonight," Bezo said as Mike exited the door.

Reaching the hallway, Mike said with a smile.

Mike repeated this process at West Tampa Projects, ending it with collecting a large gym-sized bag of money. The day was long, with Mike dropping off work to the hustlers, and picking up money from them at the same time. After making the last step to pick up money from the hustlers in front of Sharron's corner store on Nebraska Avenue, Malaya was exhausted.

"So, what do you think, Lay-Lay?" Mike asked.

"Think about what?" Malaya looked confused.

"About the operation. So, you think you can handle all of this? You know, what we did today. Can you handle it by yourself?" asked Mike.

"I don't know. Maybe if you go over everything with me again, I could. I don't want to get in trouble," Malaya replied.

"Baby girl, there's no trouble to get into. All you have to do is drop off the work and pick the money up. It's not like you standing in front of the projects selling the shit yourself," Mike said.

"Why can't Keisha do it?"

Mike became frustrated with Malaya. "Because that bitch is greedy. She don't know how to take her slice of the pie and enjoy

it. And plus, when it comes to other niggas with money, I can't trust her to keep her legs closed. And a bitch with open legs, is a bitch that can't be trusted."

"Mike, I'm not going to sit here and let you talk about my sister like she's a fucking hoe," Malaya said, becoming angry at Mike and the comment he made about Keisha.

"My bad, baby girl, but the truth is the truth," Mike said firmly.

Malaya really couldn't say anything. Lately, Keisha had been conducting herself like a hoe. She just stared out the window watching the buildings go by.

"Let's swing by your house, and recount this money," Mike said, looking at Malaya. Mike was going to use this time to find out why Malaya left him nine years ago when she was attending Morgan State University. Even though Mike was mad at Malaya for running out on him with his unborn child, he was still in love with her. Deep down, he knew she was the only woman he had ever loved. He knew the only way he could get close to Malaya was by trying to get her on his team, moving work for him throughout the city of Tampa.

Malaya exited the car and got that eerie feeling again that someone was watching them.

I really need to get some rest, Malaya thought. *Lack of sleep is making me paranoid.*

Grabbing the bags out the back seat of the car, Mike followed Malaya to the front door of her house, watching her ass move from side to side. Getting excited, he just kept thinking back to when he used to have his dick buried deep in Malaya's tight, wet pussy.

Wasting no time, Mike dumped all the money out of the bags onto Malaya's coffee table. Malaya's heart skipped a beat when she saw all that money on the table. She had never seen so much money at one time before in her life. Not wanting Mike to see that look in her eyes. She grabbed the remote off the table and hit the play button. Floetry's "It's Getting Late" played softly from the entertainment system speakers.

"Lay-Lay, what do you know about Floetry?" Mike asked.

"I got hip to Floetry from Velli." Just the mere mention of Velli put an uneasy mood in the room.

"Here," Mike said, handing Malaya a stack of bills.

"What's this for?" Malaya asked, taking the money from Mike.

"Just a little something extra for helping me out today."

"Thanks Mike, but I did not do anything but ride around with you."

"And look so damn fine doing it, too."

Mike caught Malaya off-guard by the comment. She just rolled her eyes and said, "Let's get this money counted so I can go to bed and get some rest."

"Okay, baby girl, but before we start can I ask you a couple of questions?"

"Sure, why not?" Malaya said, getting a little impatient with Mike.

"Do you really love that nigga Velli?"

Malaya looked straight into his eyes and said without a shadow of doubt, "I love Velli. My sun rises and sets with my husband. He can never and will never be replaced."

Hearing Malaya's passion for another man made a fire burn in the pit of Mike's stomach.

"What happened to us? What happened to our unborn child, Malaya?" Mike asked.

Hearing the last question made Malaya's eyes start to water, but before she shed tears, the doorbell rang. Snatching the door open. Malaya was shocked to see Keisha standing there with hate in her eyes.

"What the fuck Mike's car doing in your driveway?" Keisha screamed.

Malaya was at a loss for words. Before she could respond, Mike leaped up off the couch to confront Keisha.

"Bitch, who the fuck do you think you are? You don't walk your ass in nobody's house askin' shit about me, you got that? We are talking about business that doesn't concern you. I was on my way

to your spot anyway, so hop yo' ass in that Benz I paid for and follow me." Keisha tucked her tail and headed to the door, but not before she threw Malaya a menacing look.

Keisha sat in her car, scowling and thinking about the way Mike dotes over Malaya, like she was some fragile China doll. She thought, I *know that bitch is up to something, prancing around my man unveiled. Wonder what your precious Velli would think about his bitch now? That bitch wouldn't know half the shit she knows if it wasn't for me. I am the one that brought her in this game. I gave her this work. One thing I know for sure, I am the bitch who always comes out on top. I will make damn sure of that. When the opportunity presents itself, I will break that bitch down to size.*

Jibril Williams

CHAPTER 10

AN ANGEL'S DEMISE

It amazed Malaya how much money she had managed to make in just a few short months. She already had enough to put the thirty thousand down for Velli's lawyers and pay her car off, along with a few other credit cards. It felt amazing to hand Anya a cashier's check for ten thousand to help pay for a nurse so A'idah could get the best care at home. Malaya told Anya a little white lie about how she got the money to help pay for A'idah's care. She told Anya she'd cashed in one of her bonds. What was even more shocking was that Malaya had managed to bank all of the money and keep it a secret from everyone.

Despite the tension that had been growing between Malaya and Keisha, they both put the bullshit aside and came together to try to plan a birthday party for little A'idah.

"Anya, what do you think about getting A'idah a clown for her birthday? You know that girl loves clowns," Malaya said.

"Hmmmm. I really don't know. The doctor said A'idah has a very weak immune system, so it's best to keep A'idah away from other children."

"Yeah, you're right. I forgot about that," Malaya said with a frown, though she was determined to get A'idah a clown.

"Okay, I got it! Why don't we have A'idah's birthday on Skype?" Keisha said. "I can have all of A'idah's friends come over here for the party and hook the Skype up on my seventy-five-inch through the computer. And Malaya, you can do the same at your house."

"Keisha, you are a genius! We can have two cakes and two clowns. It'll be a cake and a clown here at your house, and one at my house," Malaya said, getting excited about the idea Keisha came up with.

"So, you telling me that we are going to have two parties at two different places for one little girl?" Anya questioned.

"Yes!" Keisha and Malaya shouted excitedly.

"Okay. I just want my baby to be happy," Anya said as she left the room to go check on A'idah, who was watching TV in Keisha's den.

"Oh, shoot!" Malaya said as she noticed the clock and saw it was 10:00 pm. She knew she had to get home so she could get up early to go see Velli. "Let me get going. I forgot I have to take Anya and A'idah home."

"Anya, come on, let's go! It's getting late. You know we gotta get our beauty rest so we can go see the hubbies tomorrow!" Malaya yelled to Anya.

"Are you going to see Dinkles tomorrow?" Malaya asked Keisha.

"I don't know, girl. I got so much other shit I need to do."

"What could be more important than going to see your husband? Keisha, you haven't seen your husband in a month. He's been asking Velli to ask me about you. I hate to lie to my husband for you."

"What's wrong? You've been lying to Velli," Keisha retorted with her hands on her hips and fire in her eyes.

Just before Malaya could check Keisha and put her in place, Anya entered the room with A'idah. "We are ready," Anya announced, sensing the tension in the room.

"Okay." Malaya picked up her purse and keys off the table.

"As Salaamu Alaikum!" Anya said to Keisha as she walked out the front door.

"Salaam, sister. I hope to see you tomorrow at visitation, if you can roll your ass out of Mikey's bed early enough," Malaya whispered to Keisha.

"Hmph. We'll see. Maybe I'll bring Mike with me. I am sure you can remember how good that dick was," Keisha said with a smirk on her face as she watched Malaya walk out the door.

Malaya was in shock. *What does this bitch know about me and Mike?* she wondered.

As soon as A'idah head hit the back seat of Malaya's car, she was out like a light. "Anya, look at her," Malaya said, eyeing A'idah through her rear-view mirror.

"Yeah, my little angel must be tired."

"Why don't you and A'idah spend the night at my house? We both got to go see our husbands tomorrow morning anyway, and you know you and A'idah got clean clothes already at my house," Malaya said.

"Okay, that sounds like a plan," Anya agreed.

Pulling up in front of Malaya's house, Malaya wasted no time helping Anya get little sleeping A'idah out the back seat of the car.

"Malaya, go open the door. I can carry A'idah in by myself," Anya said, following close behind Malaya with the sleeping A'idah in her arms.

As Malaya unlocked her front door and walked in her house, she smelled cigarette smoke, and she knew right then something was wrong. Before she could react, a savage blow struck the left side of her face, knocking her to the floor.

"Bitch, get the fuck in here! I've been waiting for your ass," the masked man said while standing over Malaya.

Catching Anya off-guard, the other gunman grabbed her by the back of her hijab and pointed his gun into her face. "Don't move or I'll put a hole in your head the size of a half-dollar." Anya froze with fear as she watched a pool of blood ooze from Malaya's head.

"Put the little girl on the couch and lay the fuck on the floor beside your homegirl." Doing what the gunman said, Anya placed the sleeping A'idah on the couch, and laid beside Malaya on the floor. "Now where's the fucking money stash at?" Hearing this, Anya told the gunmen the money was in their purses. After snatching the purses off the floor and going through them, the tallest gunman went off.

"Bitch, you think we playing with that ass?" He grabbed Malaya up by her hair and started slamming his fist into her face over and over, knocking her out with one blow and waking her up with another. Anya watched in horror.

"Please, stop! We don't have any money!"

The gunman stopped beating Malaya. "Bitch, I came to get some money and I'm not leaving until I do."

"I will fuck this little bitch if you don't tell me where the money is stashed!" He taunted Anya over his shoulder, while traumatizing little A'idah with his penis.

"Come on, man! What the fuck you doing? I'm not with fucking with no kids, nigga! Let's get that bread and bounce the fuck outta here," the short gunman complained.

"Please don't hurt my baby. You can have me. Take me, please! She's just a little girl," Anya pleaded.

"I think I will sample them goods, bitch," he remarked while kicking Anya in the side. "Roll over on your stomach!" Anya did as she was told.

"Please don't hurt her!" Malaya cried, laying a few feet away from Anya.

The tall gunman dropped his pants to his ankles, exposing his long, fat dick. He dropped down onto his knees and spat a glob of spit into the crack of Anya's ass cheeks. Anya cried out in pain as the gunman pushed into her anus with excruciating force.

"Aggghhhhh! Oh God, no!"

"Yo' God isn't here right now, bitch! It's just me and this dick here." Slamming farther into Anya's ass, Anya cried in pain. She tried to mentally escape from reality as her ass got ripped from the punishment the gunman was putting on her. The more he violated her, the more blood and shit oozed from her ass. All she could do was focus on the strange tattoo he had on his hand. That was a tattoo she would never forget.

"Come on, man! Get the fuck up and let's go. There's no money in this bitch," the shotgun man said as he snatched his partner from on top of Anya.

"Man, these whore ass bitches know where the money is," the tall gunman said in a fit of rage.

"If they had the money, they would have given it up by now," the short gunman shot back at his partner.

"If the money ain't here, then I'm fucking everything in here, including the little girl."

"I'm not going to let you fuck that little girl."

"Who da fuck is going to stop me?" the tall gunman said as he pointed his gun at his partner.

"Man, are you going to point your piece at me?" The short gun man rushed his partner and grabbed his arm, which held the gun.

"What the fuck is you doing, nicca?" The tall gunman questioned as they struggled for the gun. Getting the best of shorty, he fell on top of him, but shorty wasn't going down easy. He twisted his partner's arm, keeping the gun pointed away from him. Just as the tall gunman was gaining a better position on shorty, the gun discharged. *Boom*!

That lone bullet was destined to meet its target. It pierced A'idah's left temple and exited just as quickly as it entered. The impact forced A'idah's head to thrust forward in the direction of Anya and Malaya. Everyone froze as A'idah's eyes instantly focused on her two favorite people, her Ummi and Malaya. She seemed to silently say goodbye as one solitary tear streamed down her face. Her eyes became glassy and death consumed her.

Anya and Malaya scramble to get to A'idah, but not before they are swiftly dealt with. Lights out.

CHAPTER 11

WHO'S TO BLAME?

Every inch of Anya's body hurt. She was lying face-down in a hospital bed, her body riddled with stitches, cuts, and bruises. She kept on replaying the scene over and over again in her head. She remembered the masked man making reference to Mike hiding his stash over at Malaya's house. *That just doesn't make sense*, Anya thought, *why would the nigga Keisha is screwing be keeping his stash at Malaya's? What type of shit has Malaya gotten herself into?*

Anya heard Malaya moaning as she laid just a few feet away from her in a nearby hospital bed. They both should be thankful to be alive. Ironically, Anya was not.

"They should have killed me when they took my baby away from me."

"What did you say?" Malaya did not realize that Anya had regained consciousness yet.

"I said, they should have killed me when they took my baby from me," Anya repeated, even more maliciously than she had stated before.

"Anya, listen to me."

"No, you listen to me. I am not as stupid or as naive as you and Keisha may think I am. I know the two of you are into some shit way over your heads. And up until now, I had been minding my own business. But the choices you two have made took my baby away from me. You better believe someone will pay!" Anya began to sob uncontrollably.

Malaya would give anything to wrap her arms around Anya and comfort her right now, but numerous broken bones prevented her from doing so. Malaya decided she would tell Anya everything and she did.

Anaya laid in shock as she listened to her best friend tell her about the secret life she had been living for the last few months. Pools of tears formed in Anya's hospital bed as she realized her best friend had turned into someone she no longer recognized.

After listening to Malaya, it was clear to Anya that what she was about to say to Malaya would probably ruin their friendship for life. Then again, for Anya, life had ceased to exist without A'idah.

"Malaya, I think it is best that you know my intentions. I have no desire to live, and I plan to kill the mutherfuckas that killed my baby." Malaya was taken aback by Anya's use of such harsh language. "In two days, I will bury my only child, and when they shovel that last bit of dirt onto her eternal resting place, I will kill Keisha. Then I will find Mike, but before I kill him, I will kill everyone he loves. I just hope you are not one of those he loves."

"Wait! Anya, Mike and I are old news. I just needed him to get the money I need for Velli. But what does Keisha have to do with this?"

"You have been naive to Keisha and her ways for far too long. And if you stand by this bitch, you will go down with her too. Do you think this lifestyle you have created for yourself is easy to get out of? You are a fool if you think so."

"I know Keisha has a lot of issues, but she is still our sister!" Malaya tried her best to convince Anya. This was not the Anya she knew. She was different now. Death tends to do that to people. Malaya reflected back to the last image she had of A'idah and was consumed with grief. She knew Anya was right. Someone, everyone must pay for A'idah's death. Malaya just wasn't so sure Keisha was to blame.

CHAPTER 12

SAYING GOODBYE

Two days later...

The funeral was packed with friends and family paying their respects to baby A'idah. The marshals arrived with Muhammad in tow. He walked towards baby A'idah, to bid farewell to his only daughter. Reminiscing of times spent with A'idah, Malaya started to slowly unravel. Feeling someone staring at her, she looked over to see Muhammad pleading with his eyes, saying, "Please take care of my wife." Malaya nodded, acknowledging his request.

As Muhammad exited the funeral, he turned to see Malaya rushing to aid his wife who was draped over his daughter's body, refusing to depart with her only child. Muhammad hoped for some compassion from the marshals, just hoping that they would allow him to comfort his wife, but of course they did not. He was ushered out just as swiftly as he'd entered.

***

Velli sat in his eight by twelve cell, staring at the walls in silence, waiting impatiently for Muhammad to return from A'idah's funeral. *It's almost time for the four o'clock count, and he should have been back by now*, Velli thought. Thinking about the tragic event that claimed baby A'idah's life caused Velli's eyes to become laden with tears as he said a prayer for her. "Oh, Allah, you are the most great, the Most High. You created all things and all things shall return to you. Please be kind to baby A'idah and grant her a special place in your paradise, Ameen."

Just as Velli was ending his prayer, the C.O. was unlocking the cell door to let Muhammad back into the cell. "As Salaam Alaikum."

"Wa Alaikum Salaam," Velli replied back to Muhammad, embracing him in a brotherly hug. He hugged Muhammad a little

tighter and a few seconds longer, to let his brother know he was there from him, and that he felt his pain to the core.

Releasing his comrade from his embrace, Muhammad immediately removed his shoes to begin cleaning his face, hands, and feet to perform his noon prayer he had missed while he was gone to the funeral. Velli was dying inside to ask Muhammad if he had a chance to talk to anybody at the funeral to get some type of insight as to what took place dealing with the home invasion and the shooting of baby A'idah.

"I've been calling Keisha ever since this morning."

"And?" Muhammad said as he wiped the water from his face and feet with this towel.

"Brother, she's not talking. She keeps saying that she doesn't know what happened and she's just happy that she did not have to witness the madness. I can feel that she's holding something back. She is too laid back about the situation." Velli gritted his teeth, frustrated with Keisha playing stupid. "Then this bitch had the nerve to tell me to stop calling her house, questioning her like I'm her man."

"What did Abdul Hakeem say when he called Keisha and asked about what happened with our families?" Muhammad asked, referring to Dinkles by his real name.

"She just told him she was not in the mood to talk about it."

Muhammad ran his hand over his face and beard, taking in what Velli was telling him. Velli caught himself venting. Knowing that Muhammad was in a much worse situation than him, given that he lost a child, Velli apologized to him. "I'm sorry, brother."

"I understand, Velli. I know you are worried about your wife. Have you talked to her yet?"

"No," Velli said, taking a deep breath, becoming more worried because he hasn't talked to his wife yet. Malaya was avoiding his calls. He had his brother, Damu, try to locate her but he had no luck.

"You know, Velli, Allah is the greatest. I was supposed to have twenty minutes with my daughter alone, but the marshals got lost twice on our way to the funeral, and when we finally made it there, the funeral was packed. I did not get a chance to say anything to

anybody. But I must confess though, Akri (brother) Malaya was almost unrecognizable."

"What the fuck you mean she was almost unrecognizable?"

Velli slammed his right hand into his cell wall with such force, his hand instantly swelled. "I'm going to kill whoever had something to do with this," Velli yelled out. The thought that the same motherfucker mishandled his wife was too much for him. It sent him over the top.

"Trust me, brother, I'm going to be right by your side when that day comes," Muhammad confirmed with a murderous look on his face.

Days later...

Velli anxiously paced his cell, waiting for Malaya. He had finally spoken to her, and upon her release form the hospital, she was coming to see him. He was eager to hold and comfort his wife. His blood was boiling over the tragic events that had taken place. The mere thought of someone violating his wife and his home was unbearable. Even when Velli was in the streets, he always had compassion for women and children. Never would he have hurt a child. Never. Who could have looked into A'idah's beautiful chestnut eyes and blown her brains out? Who would do such a thing?

Velli had called Keisha numerous times, trying to get an update on Malaya and Anya and every time he talked to her, she seemed annoyed he was even calling. Something was going on, but he just couldn't put his finger on it. On top of all of that, he felt like he didn't even know Malaya anymore. People had warned him that when men get locked up, their women change. He always hoped it would not be true for his queen.

He was still disturbed by the visit he had with his brother and replayed the citation over and over again in his mind. Damu said he went over to Malaya's to retrieve his cell phone, only to find Malaya leaving the house unveiled, with some drug dealin' nigga named Mike. No matter what the reason, to Velli, this was the ultimate betrayal.

Jibril Williams

CHAPTER 13

EXPOSED

Malaya waited nervously as the prison guard processed her paperwork to visit Velli. The guard gave her a strange look, asking why her face was covered with cuts and bruises. She lied and said, "Car accident." Seemingly satisfied with her answer, the guard allowed her to proceed to the visitation room.

Velli entered the visitation room and his heart sank. His queen was barely recognizable. All he could do before words were spoken was to wrap his arms around her and plant gentle kisses all over her face. Velli's eyes were burning with emotion, but with limited time for visitation, he knew that he must quickly find out what was going on.

"Malaya, from the beginning to now, tell me what happened."

"Well, Anya, A'idah and I had just left Keisha's house, where we were discussing the plans for A'idah's birthday party. Anya and A'idah were going to spend the night with me, so we could ride to visitation together the next morning. I opened the front door and that's when..." Malaya couldn't bear to finish her sentence. Every time she mentioned A'idah's name, a part of her died.

"Baby, calm down. Please stop crying."

"Okay. When I went into the house, I knew something wasn't right. I smelled cigarette smoke. Before I knew what was happening, I was struck from the side." Malaya could not bring herself to tell Velli they cut her clothes off, nor could she tell him how they violated Anya or A'idah. "I regained consciousness, right around the time they shot A'idah."

"What made them shoot her?" Velli inquired.

"I-I think I remember hearing one of the robbers say she would be able to identify them, and they didn't want any witnesses," Malaya lied.

But they weren't worried 'bout you and Anya being able to identify them?"

"Well, right after they hit me the first time, they blindfolded me and Anya…" Malaya was hoping her story matched with whatever Anya told Muhammad.

"Hmmmmm, I see. So, why do you think they picked out a house to rob? I mean, it was a robbery, correct?"

"Well, yeah. Of course. I guess because they knew I was there by myself. They probably have been watching me for a while."

"I find it unusual that robbers would break into a house with the intention to rob it, but instead they decide to murder a child, brutally beat two women, and leave with nothing." Velli's blood was beginning to boil. He was hoping Malaya would just tell him the truth, but just like most common bitches, she chose to lie. Malaya began to sob and cry uncontrollably. "Not this time, Malaya. This is your last chance to tell me the truth. I need the story from the beginning. The real beginning, starting with the man Damu saw you get into the car with."

Malaya took a deep breath and prepared to bear her soul. "You are right. I got desperate. I knew I would never be able to legally afford the kind of lawyer you need, so when I was presented with the opportunity to make some quick money, I took it," Malaya explained.

"And who presented you with the opportunity? Mike?"

Dammit! How the hell does he know his name? Shit, shit, shit! "Well, not exactly. Mike is a friend of Keisha's and—"

"Hold up!" Velli interrupted. "A friend of Keisha's? Does Dinkles know about Keisha's friend? Never mind. Hell no, he doesn't know! Continue with your story."

"Keisha's friend, Mike, needed someone to transport his drugs for him from Texas and to pick up his drops around the city. It was quick and easy money, and that's how I paid the retainer for the lawyer."

"So, the whole business about you getting a personal loan was a lie then too, huh?" Velli inquired.

"Yes, but I didn't want you to worry. I—"

"Hold up! My wife is transporting narcotics for some nigga I don't even know, and you want me not to worry? What made you

trust this nigga so much? How do you know he won't turn up evidence against you?"

"I trust him, because Keisha knows him well, and—"

"Yeah, I bet Keisha knows him well! If she trusts him so much, why don't she move his work for him then?"

Malaya didn't really want to put Keisha on blast, but there was no way out of this. "Keisha works for him too."

Velli was at a loss for words. It all made sense to him now. He couldn't believe his wife was in the same game he tried so hard to protect her from. No matter the outcome, she was in it now.

"Malaya, as of right now, I need some time to process all of this. No matter what, I do love you. I just need some time right now. Just know whoever did this to you, will pay. I put my life on that!"

With that, Velli abruptly stood up, kissed Malaya on the forehead, and walked out of the visitation room.

Jibril Williams

CHAPTER 14

NO CHOICE

Malaya walked sullenly out of Coleman Federal Prison, not really knowing how to take Velli's reaction. "How would you expect him to react? He is acting like any husband would. I just hope Velli sees this was done for us."

No sooner than Malaya got in the car, her cell phone was vibrating in her purse. "Hello?" Malaya's heart sank in her chest when he realized it was Velli's lawyer, Mr. McCullough.

Unfortunately, it seemed whenever he called, he had bad news, or he wanted to discuss their "payment" agreement. This time he hit her with a double whammy. The private investigator had discovered there was evidence from the "alleged" scene of Valli's crime, that had never been tested by the forensics department, and in order for the evidence to be tested, it would cost ten thousand!

That was another ten on top of the thirty thousand Malaya had already given the lawyer. So, now the lawyer was expecting Malaya to just hand over another ten just like that? It was clear to Malaya this justice system was designed to seek, capture, and destroy, and that was exactly what it was doing to her.

The lawyer sensed Malaya's apprehension and stated, "This could be the evidence we need to exonerate Velli." He knew that was all he needed to say. Slick bastard!

"I will get the ten thousand to you for the forensics, and I will get another ten-thousand-dollar-payment to you. Just give me some time. I'll call you."

Malaya pulled her car to the side of the expressway. She beat the steering wheel, shouting, "Now what am I supposed to do? Where the fuck am I supposed to get that type of money?" Malaya knew the answers to her own questions. There was no way for her to get out of this game now. The stakes were too high. Malaya knew the next move that she would have to make was going to have to be a real money-maker move in order to generate the kind of funds she needed.

After hanging up with the lawyer, Malaya decided to call Anya to take her up on her offer to stay with her. Malaya could not bear the thought of going back to her home where A'idah was viciously murdered, and where she and Anya were savagely attacked. On the way to Anya's house, Malaya still saw the crime scene tape that covered her front door. The thought of that night sent chills through her body. Ultimately, someone would pay for the events of that night.

CHAPTER 15

HOLDING BACK

Velli exited the visitation room, trying desperately to make sense of and process the situation that caused his wife to be brutally attacked, and his dearest friend's daughter to be murdered. Thinking back on how Malaya's face looked brought tears to his eyes. *I can't believe a motherfucker did this shit to my wife*, Velli thought.

He was hoping to have some alone time to digest the things he and Malaya just talked about, but he was sadly mistaken. Muhammad was sitting in the cell. Not saying anything to Muhammad. Velli went straight to a gym bag hanging on the foot of his bunk, grabbed his MP3 player, and changed into his workout clothes. He needed to do something to burn some frustration before he went haywire.

Velli saw Muhammad peering at him through his peripheral, but Velli couldn't make eye contact with his friend, knowing his wife's actions were what got his friend's daughter killed. There was no way in the world Velli could tell his friend the truth.

"As Salaamu Alaikum, Velli. Things with the wife were rough, huh? I see you left the visit early," Muhammad said, watching Velli's every move.

"Arki, (brother) things are worse than I thought. Alhamdulillah, (Praise Be to Allah), that I got a chance to see my wife today, but I swear by Allah, her face will haunt me until my soul is claimed. Malaya nor Anya knows who robbed them or how it was A'idah was killed. Malaya couldn't tell me much about what happened. She was knocked out most of the time when the home invasion was going on. She came to not long before A'idah was shot."

Muhammad sensed that Velli was holding something back, but he decided not to push the issue. "I keep hearing our wives were raped. Is this true?" Did Malaya say anything about this?"

"I got it from one of Anya's cousins, but the girl is a known liar, so it may not be trusted at all."

The information wrecked Velli. "The next time I see Malaya, I will ask her about this."

Velli realized that he was not able to stay in Muhammad's presence much longer. "Look, brother, I got to go clear my head and they just called the activity move. We will talk later." Velli gave Muhammad a pound and left the cell.

CHAPTER 16

OUT OF THE GAME

Malaya disconnected her call, threw her cell phone in the passenger seat and pounded the steering wheel again in frustration. Malaya knew she needed time to mourn A'idah's death before she would be ready to jump back into the game, and Mike seemed to understand this, until now. Mike was acting like some love-sick boyfriend trying to protect his sweetheart, which Malaya was not. Mike claimed he felt the need to protect Malaya. Protection wasn't what Malaya needed. She needed money. Malaya had a feeling Keisha was behind all of this. It would be just like her to cut Malaya out of her money.

Right on cue, Keisha called Malaya. "As Salaamu Alaikum, sis!"

"Wa Alaikum," Malaya replied dryly.

"What's wrong, girl? Mike just called me and said he feels it is best to keep you out of the game for now. He said he tried to explain that to you, and you got mad and hung up on him. I have to agree with Mike, girl. I think it is for the best for right now. You were involved in a horrific situation, and you need time to heal," Keisha explained.

"Funny you say that, because while I am healing, you out there making all the damn money!"

Keisha was thrown off by Malaya's brash tone. "Hold up, I still gots to make my money! I got a lifestyle I got to uphold." Keisha realized she might have gone a little too far. "Listen, I know what you need. You and Anya just need to get out for a while. Let's have a girls' day, my treat! Be ready in an hour and I will come by Anya's to pick you both up."

Malaya hung up and immediately called Anya, expecting her to deny Keisha's invitation. On the contrary, Malaya was shocked that Anya was willing to see Keisha and spend the entire day with her.

"I would love to hang out today! A girls' day is exactly what I need!" Anya exclaimed. *Besides, I need to get close to Keisha. It is about time I find out what that bitch really knows!*

"Okay, well I am almost back at your house. Keisha says to be ready in an hour."

CHAPTER 17

ANYA'S PLOT

Malaya stood in the shower at Anya's house, still puzzled by Anya's eagerness to hang out with Keisha. She hadn't had much to do with Keisha since the events of that tragic night that took A'idah away from her. "Anya is my sister till the end, but she has something up her sleeve," Malaya pondered aloud, while stepping out of the shower.

"Malaya, Keisha just called. She is pulling up now!" Anya shouted to Malaya as she walked towards the living room, grabbing her purse.

"Okay. I'm coming!" Malaya quickly threw on a jogging suit and headed towards the living room. Malaya stopped dead in the tracks when she saw Anya. "Where is your hijab? Why aren't you covered up!"

Anya just shrugged her shoulders. "I just felt like doing something different today." Anya knew Keisha would respond to her differently when she was out of her Islamic dress. She was determined to find out everything Keisha knew by any means necessary.

Malaya was still sensing that Anya was up to something, but now was not the time to question her. "Are you sure about this, Anya?"

"I have never been surer about anything in my life," Anya replied with sheer determination.

Beep! Beep!

Keisha grew impatient. "What is taking them so damn long?" As the two emerged, Keisha could see what had been taking so long. She was in utter shock at the sight of Anya uncovered. Keisha was speechless for the moment.

"Allah, please protect me from the likes of Shaytan (Satan)," Anya whispered, while she glared stonily at Keisha.

"Now girl, dat's what I'm talking 'bout! It's about time you show the world what you got to offer!" Keisha announced.

A short while later, Keisha pulled up at Citrus Park Mall. "Why did you pick to come to this mall way out here?" Before Keisha could answer Malaya's question, three guys started walking up to the driver's side window and greeted Keisha. Overly paranoid, Malaya's initial reaction was to jump out the car and run, but something seemed vaguely familiar about one of the guys. She thought she had seen him before.

Two of the guys stood back, while the tallest of the three guys approached Keisha's driver's side window. Given Keisha's eagerness, this must have been a planned meeting. The grin on Keisha's face and the way she was squirming in her seat and nibbling on her bottom lip, told Malaya all she needed to know. Whoever this guy was, he was obviously fucking Keisha.

Malaya took a sideways glance and looked at Anya in the backseat. Anya was staring at the man while he leaned over in the driver's side window and tongued Keisha down. Keisha ran her right hand down in between her legs and stroked her pussy while they continued their tonguing escapade. Sensing the tension in the car, the guy broke the kiss and looked over at Malaya. Once their eyes met, she recognized him as the guy she met with Mike. *What is his name*? Malaya thought.

"My bad, ladies. I shouldn't be so rude. This is my new boo, Redz," Keisha informed.

This bitch really is crazy. She has the game so fucked up. First, she is fucking Mike, and now she is fucking one of his boys. She is really playing with fire. Does Mike know? Malaya wondered all of this in silence.

Malaya decided not to let on that Mike had already introduced her to Redz. "Nice to meet you, Redz."

When Redz leaned in the car across Keisha to shake Malaya's hand, Anya let out the most gut-wrenching gasp ever heard. Keisha and Redz were so engrossed in each other, they didn't seem to notice. But Malaya did. Looking at Anya's face, Malaya knew something was terribly wrong. Sensing Anya was not really ready for this "girls' day out," Malaya thought fast and came up with an excuse to take Anya back home.

76

Malaya grabbed her purse. "Awww, fuck! My bad, Keisha, take me back to Anya's house. I must have dropped my wallet getting in your car. My cash, ID, and everything is in there!"

Keisha was pissed that her rendezvous with Redz was short-lived, but happy when he handed her a stack of bills and tongued her down again, before walking away and promising to hook up with her later.

Back at Anya's house, Malaya hopped out of Keisha's car and Anya quickly followed. Keisha gave Anya a puzzled look when she immediately rushed in the house and made no attempt to help Malaya look for her wallet.

Malaya pulled her wallet out of her purse and tossed it along the sidewalk, out of Keisha's view. "Girl. I found it! Here it is by the bushes! I'mma run in the house and tell Anya I found it. I will be right back!" Malaya called out to Keisha, who was still sitting in the car.

Malaya walked in the house to find Anya crying hysterically, and she knew Anya was not ready to mingle with the world just yet. She was still in mourning. Malaya returned to Keisha's car. "Well, it looks like you can hook up with your new boo, sooner than later."

"Why, what's up with Anya?" Keisha questioned like she was really concerned.

"She just isn't really up to hanging out yet. She is still mourning A'idah. We will hook up with you soon. Promise."

"A'ight girl. Hollatcha later." Keisha eagerly pulled off, with her pussy throbbing at the thought of Redz plunging his fat dick inside of her. *They just don't know...those bitches just made my night*!

Jibril Williams

CHAPTER 18

VIOLATED

Maybe it was too soon for Anya to come out. Maybe she needs more time to mourn, Malaya thought. *I can't imagine the pain that she's gone through right now.* Malaya hugged Anya, wishing she could hug all of her pain away.

Breaking her embrace, Anya looked at Malaya and said, "I know you probably think I'm crazy, but I'm not. There are some things about that night I will never forget. One thing I will never forget is the man who took my life from me. I know *him*, Malaya. I know his mannerisms, I know his voice, but most importantly I know his tattoo, the one on his hand."

At first, Malaya thought Anya was rambling, but then she said, "Wait. What did you say about a tattoo?"

"The man that raped me, beat you, and killed my baby, had the strangest-looking tattoo on his hand. It was hard to make out what it was that night. It almost looks satanic, but whatever it was, I knew I would always remember it. I saw the same tattoo tonight."

Malaya slumped down in a heap on the floor and placed her face in her hands. Was it the same tattoo on the guy Redz we saw tonight?"

"Yes, and now I know that bitch Keisha had something to do with all of this! It would just be too much of a coincidence! That bitch took my baby away from me. You can't tell me she isn't involved. First, she is fucking Mike, and we almost got killed behind an attempted robbery, by someone trying to get his money. Then, she is fucking the dude that committed the robbery and killed *my* baby!

"Is all of this sinking into you, Malaya? Or are you still going to deny Keisha's involvement in all of the thirst?" Anya was furious. "Think about it, Malaya. The detective clearly stated that there was no forced entry! That means the person had to have a key! Who else has a key to your house, other than me?"

Keisha. Malaya needed time to process all of this, it was just too much right now. Her head was pounding. "Anya, are you sure that was the tattoo you saw that night? That tattoo on Redz is the *same* one you saw that night?" Malaya still needed confirmation.

"That is not something I would or could ever forget, Malaya! My baby's last image of me was seeing a vile man ramming his dick into my ass. I was too ashamed to look at my daughter. All I had to stare at was his hands as he gripped the floor for more leverage while he savagely raped me! So, hell yeah, I am sure!"

The next day...

Malaya sat in the car alone, in front of Keisha's house, going over the things she and Anya talked about the day before. "I can't believe Keisha had something to do with my house getting robbed." With tears sliding down her cheeks, Malay was thinking about the horrendous night that claimed baby A'idah's life and violated Anya to no return.

"I got to confront this bitch to see what she knows about the murder and robbery, or at least try to pick her for information. I just can't believe my girl had something to do with this shit, but Anya is right. She's been playing it too cool, too damn laid back when her friend just lost a child and could have been killed. Oh Allah, please don't let this be so," Malaya prayed as she exited her car. Walking into Keisha's house, Malaya could hear Melanie Fiona's song, "It Kills Me," softly coming through Keisha's speakers.

"Keisha, it's Malaya. As Salaam Alaikum!"

"Hey, girl!" Keisha replied while waking into the living room, damn near naked. Seeing her like this made Malaya turn her head.

Keisha's slightly shaved pussy was visible through her lacy, baby blue boy shorts. Keisha loved when she had the opportunity to be exposed in front of Malaya, like she was now.

"What brings you over, girl?" Keisha asked, adjusting her bra to make her titties look plumper than they already were. "Is your girl, Anya, still tripping?"

"Naw. She just has a lot on her mind right now." Malaya tried not to make eye contact with Keisha. "I just came over to see how you were doing."

"Well, I'm doing good, as you can plainly see. I just got some company coming over. You see I gots my music playing, my candles burning, and my champagne on ice. All I'm waiting on is Mike to get here and it's on and poppin'!' Keisha swayed her hips to the beat of the music. Just hearing Mike's name made Malaya remember why she came by Keisha's house in the first place.

"Oh, girl, I had been meaning to ask you. I lost my house key. Do you still have the extra set of keys I gave you?"

"Naw, girl. I lost them keys a few months back," Keisha replied while turning her back on Malaya and walking towards the kitchen. "You want something to drink, Malaya?"

"Yeah, girl. Some juice would be fine."

Hearing Keisha no longer had her keys made it even easier to convict her of having something to do with the murder and robbery. The police said there wasn't any forced entry. *Either I left the door unlocked or the robbers got in through an unlocked window, but that is not like me to leave a window unlocked*, Malaya thought. *That's bullshit. Anya is right. Keisha must have given my key to Redz in order for them to get in my house.*

"Keisha, how long have you been messing around with Redz?" Hearing this made Keisha stop what she was doing in the kitchen.

"Why did you ask me about Redz, Malaya?"

"I'm just asking because I saw him a few times with Mike." Instantly, Keisha was enraged at the thought of Malaya and Mike spending time together.

"Well, I met him through Mike. He is just my little side piece when Mike is acting funny with his shit. That's all."

Malaya knew that was a lie. Keisha sensed something was wrong with Malaya. *This bitch ain't never questioned me about who I been kickin' it with. It's about time someone questions this goody-two-shoes bitch about who she's been fucking.* Keisha saw an opportunity and she seized it.

Mulling over the reality that Keisha nearly got her killed, Malaya put her head in her hands, took a deep breath and moaned, "Keisha, what the fuck have you done?"

"What did you say, girl?" Hearing Keisha's voice so close to her made her jump.

"Girl, I didn't say anything," Malaya whispered through clenched teeth and grabbed a glass of orange juice from her and took a big gulp. Keisha walked over to the corner table, grabbed a well-twisted cigar and put a fire to it. It was burning Malaya's insides at the thought that Keisha was involved with the robbery. She took another gulp of her juice.

"So, are you fucking Redz and does Mike know about it?"

"Girl, who the fuck you think you are, coming into my house and asking me about who I'm fucking? Are you fucking Mike?"

"Hell no!" Malaya shouted, shocked at how Keisha was flipping the script on her.

"Would you like to fuck Mike?" Keisha pressed on.

"Gir-girl! You are crazy about it…" Malaya was starting to feel a little funny. "Keisha put that weed out, I think I got a contact from it."

"The only thing you got a contact from is Mike?"

Malaya tried to stand up, preparing to cuss Keisha out, but when she tried her legs buckled, and she fell back on the couch.

What's wrong with me? "Keisha, hel-help me," Malaya managed to mutter. Her eyes were getting heavy.

"I'm going to help you all right," Keisha said while sliding out of her boy shirts. The last thing that Malaya saw was Keisha's slightly shaved pussy standing in front of her, before her heavy eyelids fell shut.

Keisha laid Malaya down on the couch and stripped all of her clothes off. She stood there, admiring Malaya's perky titties and her fat pussy lips. Keisha stuck two fingers in Malaya's mouth and then used those same two fingers to stroke her own erect clit. Keisha's pussy longed to feel Malaya's tongue. Not wasting any time, Keisha straddled Malaya's face, and began grinding her pussy eagerly into Malaya's face.

Not wanting to cum inside of Keisha, he slid his dick out and pulled Keisha from in between Malaya's legs. Keisha didn't put up a fight. Her place was to show Mike how much of a hoe Malaya was anyway, so that way he would stop fucking with her and see her for what she really was. As Mike leaned over Malaya, he could tell she was on some type of drug, but at the moment he didn't give a fuck. Their past came back to him, and in a rage, the thought of leaving him all those years ago came flooding back to him.

Malaya should have been his wife. She should have loved him enough to have stayed and been a mother to their unborn child. She betrayed him. The madder he got, the harder his dick became. Pushing the head of his dick into Malaya made her cry out in pain and pleasure. It had been a long time since she had some dick. She wrapped her legs around Mike and grabbed his ass, screaming, "Fuck me!"

Mike did just that. As he plunged deep inside of her, Malaya cried out, "Oh baby, please fuck me!" Mike pulled out the head of his manhood and slammed into Malaya, clenching his ass cheeks as he tried to get to the bottom of Malaya's wet pussy. Picking up speed, Mike repeatedly slammed his dick into Malaya with no mercy.

"Is this what you want? Is this what you want, Lay-Lay?"

"Oh, yes! Give it to me, Velli!" Hearing Velli's name while he was inside of her, drove Mike mad and his emotions got the best of him. Mike snatched Malaya's legs from around him and threw them over his shoulders. Mike slid his dick back into Malaya, but this time with so much force that it made her eyes roll to the back of her head.

"Awwwwwww, shit! Ooooooohhhhhhhh shit!" Malaya yelled. Keisha sat back and watched the brutal fucking, recording every move with her cell phone.

"Why the fuck you leave me? Huh? Why are you leaving me?" Mike yelled, while slamming into Malaya with such force. "Why the fuck did you kill our baby?" With clenched teeth, Mike slammed harder, trying to bust Malaya's cherry wide open.

As Keisha sat dumbfounded, hearing the truths flowing freely out of Mike's mouth, tears rolled quietly down her face. Keisha hated Malaya with a passion now. *All this time, Malaya and Mike had a history.*

"Deeper, Velli! Deeper, baby!" Harder and harder, Mike fucked Malaya out of pure hatred for Velli.

Feeling himself about to cum, Mike leaned forward and yelled in Malaya's face. "This is my pussy and it's always going to be! Grrrrrrrrrrr!" Mike let out a grunt that wasn't known to man as he released his load inside of Malaya. He laid there, letting every drop ooze inside of her.

Jibril Williams

CHAPTER 19

DEALS MADE

What felt like days to Malaya, had only been hours, since her sexual encounter with Keisha and Mike. She woke up moments ago on Keisha's living room floor, butt naked, with a swollen love box and a cloudy mind. Malaya slowly started to put the events together that took place between Keisha and Mike. As her thoughts came rolling back, Malaya's insides spilled out onto Keisha's carpet, as a river of tears flow from her eyes. "No, Allah. Please don't let this be true," she begged, but the truth was confirmed with the soreness that existed between her legs.

Jumping up, Malaya ran from room to room, screaming for Keisha. "Keisha, I'm going to kill you, bitch!" She grabbed the bat Keisha kept hidden behind her bathroom door, not finding Keisha anywhere in the house, Malaya took her anger out on everything she laid her eyes on in Keisha's house. She went from room to room, smashing Keisha's flat screen televisions, computers, and entertainment systems. She even destroyed the kitchen, breaking every dish and destroying the microwave.

Malaya wasn't finished yet. She went into the laundry room, grabbed two large bottles of bleach and bleached everything in the house, including every piece of clothing Keisha owned. The smell of bleach was overwhelming to Malaya, so she put her clothes on and left, promising herself that she was going to fuck Keisha's ass up the next time she saw her.

***

Now Malaya sat in her house with the lights out and a heart full of hatred. Malaya couldn't force herself to go back to Anya's house after what happened between her and Keisha. So, she went home, took a hot shower, and tried to scrub the forbidden act from her skin. She'd been avoiding everybody ever since, including Velli. She couldn't bring herself to talk to him at the moment, because Velli

would detect the distress in her voice and know something was wrong with her.

Anya had been calling non-stop, leaving messages, and asking Malaya to call her. Anya was worried about her. The bitch Keisha was even calling, threatening to whip her ass when she caught her out in the street, for what she did to her house. What made things crazy was this bitch had the nerve to say, "It's not my fault you a freak bitch! I didn't take the pussy... you gave it to me."

I cannot believe this shit," Malaya said. "All this shit happening because I wanted to make some money to help get my husband out of jail. My sister's daughter was murdered, my sister was raped in front of me, and I'm still no closer to getting my husband out of prison. I'm not going to quit. Something has got to happen in my favor. By any means, I'm going to get that money to get my husband out. I need him home with me. I'm dying without him."

The knock at the door broke Malaya's thoughts. Jumping up and grabbing a butcher knife from the kitchen, Malaya crept to the door, thinking it might have been Keisha coming to fulfill her death threats. Looking through the peephole, she saw Anya on the other side of the door. Unlocking the door and letting her in, Malaya went straight to her bedroom, not wanting to talk to Anya in the same room where her daughter got killed a few months ago.

"Salaam, sister," Anya greeted Malaya.

"Peace, Anya," Malaya let out in a whisper. Making eye contact with her dearest friend caused tears to well up in her eyes.

"What's wrong, girl?"

"You were right about Keisha having something to do with the robbery. She had something to do with A'idah's death."

Anya stepped towards Malaya. "Tell me, sister. Tell me every-thing." Malaya told Anya everything from the conversation she had with Keisha, to the threesome she had with her and Mike.

"I don't think Mike had anything to do with the robbery. Re-member they were looking for his money," Malaya recalled.

"I don't care, Malaya. I want him dead just as bad as I want Redz dead. It is his madness that caused all of this."

"But how are we going to do this, Anya?"

"We are going to use what they use to destroy nations and empires all through history."

"What's that?"

"Straight pussy." Malaya was shocked by Anya's brash tone.

"Let's make a deal. Malaya, you help me get Redz and everybody that had something to do with the death of my daughter, and I will help you do whatever it takes to get your husband home. I will help you run them drugs from Texas to Florida."

"Mike is not going to fuck with us. He is only fucking with Keisha on that tip."

"So, then, we get Keisha out of the way. It's about time she gets what is coming to her anyway," Anya said with a smile, while rubbing her hands together.

Jibril Williams

CHAPTER 20

VENGEANCE

The individuals in the black Ford Taurus had been watching Keisha's movements for the last three and a half weeks. Every Thursday night, she went to the Spa of Goddess for a full body treatment from 7:30 pm to 9:00 pm, and on Fridays she spent the day getting her manicure, pedicure, and her hair done. Their palms become sweaty as the individuals in the Taurus reflected on Keisha's betrayal. This was it. There was no turning back now. Too much had been lost. Too many lines of disrespect had been crossed, with false loyalty and greenbacks tonight, Keisha would play for her transgressions.

"Here the bitch comes now," grumbled the passenger, as Keisha walked out the Spa of Goddess. She was on her phone, feeling like a million bucks. Walking across the parking lot, feeling sexier than ever without a care in the world. Keisha was so busy talking on the phone, she didn't even see the two hooded figures creeping up behind her.

"Girl, did you see the new Jimmy Choo sandals?" the girl asked Keisha over the phone.

"Which ones are you talking about, the ones that cost two grand or the other ones?" Keisha said with a smirk.

"Bitch, you already got them?" the caller asked.

"Hell, yeah! I got them right after my threesome with Mike and that bitch—" That was all Keisha got out of her mouth, before the can of mace came around and hit her eyes with a blinding spray.

"Ah shit!" Keisha screamed out, dropping her cell phone and grabbing her face. A crushing blow came across her knee. Keisha never had a chance to defend herself or see the razor that ripped open the left side of her face. Slash after slash, Keisha's facial skin was ripped open. The more she tried to get up from the ground, the more she was cut. The assailants were not finished there, they came

prepared for revenge. They viciously swung their Louisville Slugger baseball bats into Keisha's body, instantly breaking her arms and legs.

The brutal cracks of the bats mutilated Keisha's body effortlessly. The beating was ruthless and relentless. There was no regard for human life. At some point, Keisha no longer felt the impact of the blows, she only heard the crack of her bones being broken and splintered. One final blow put Keisha out of her misery.

CHAPTER 21

VELLI'S PLAN

Velli was waiting patiently for them to bring his visitor into the visiting room. He had a lot on his mind. He needed to make some serious shit happen. He'd spoken to his lawyer, Mr. Leon McCullough. Mr. McCullough told him about the new evidence he had found in the case, and that he needed the money to have that evidence analyzed. The seed of hope planted in Velli's chest with a murderous intent.

Seeing his brother, Damu, coming through the door, brought a smile to his face. "Salaam, young blood," Velli hugged his brother.

"Peace, big bro. I see you still getting your swole on in here."

"Yeah, I got to build my weight up with my hate up and pay them back when I'm bigger. Sit down, baby boy. We got a lot to talk about." Given the intense look in Velli's eyes, Damu could sense what he was about to tell him was some serious shit.

"Look at me, Damu. I'm sitting here dying. I'm rotting away. I'm dying a broken man with a broken spirit. Most of all, I'm dying alone and of a broken heart. I want to breathe again. I want to live again, little bruh. I deserve to live again. I'm calling on you to help me. I wouldn't ask you to do anything for me I wouldn't do for you or do for myself, but right now my hands are tired. I need you to be my eyes. I need you to be my hands. I need you to untie my hands, so I can walk free from this hell hole I'm living in."

Damu nodded his head up and down. "I got you, bruh. Just tell me what you need me to do for you to make shit happen."

Looking into Damu's eyes, Velli revealed what he needed. "I need for you to get on that nigga Mike's line and find out everything you know about him. I need to know where he lays his head. I must know where he keeps his stash, not the little stash, but the big one. Once you find out everything about that nigga, murk his bitch ass. I need his money to get out of here, bruh. You feel me?"

"I got you."

"I also need you to protect my wife. She has gotten herself into a game she doesn't know how to play, but I respect her, because she got in it because of me. She knows the nigga Mike, so she might be your ticket to getting close to him. Protect her as if she was your wife, bruh."

"I'm on top of it, Velli. Don't worry."

"Damu, it's about getting that money first, then rocking that nigga to sleep. By any means, bruh."

"By any means," Damu repeated with his mind on a mission.

***

Anya drove to Malaya's house in silence. Every few blocks, she looked over at her partner in crime.

"Girl there's no need to be feeling sorry for that slimy ass bitch. She didn't feel sorry for your ass when she had your pussy in her mouth. She didn't feel sorry or have a fucking heart when that motherfucka raped my asshole and killed my daughter. Did she feel sorry then, Malaya? Did she? So, don't sit over there and feel sorry for that bitch. She got everything she deserves. I don't care if that bitch dies!" Anya screamed at Malaya.

"It's not that I feel sorry for her, it's just, I've never had anybody's blood on me before," Malaya said, staring at her clothes and bloodstained hands. As they pulled up to Malaya's house, Malaya's heart dropped when she saw Damu's red Charger sitting in the driveway. "Oh shit!"

"What, girl?" Anya said, looking around trying to figure out what's going on.

"It's Damu."

Seeing the looks on Malaya and Anya's faces, Damu knew something was wrong and it was a bad time for him to be there. "What's up, sis?" Damu greeted Malaya.

"Nothing," Malaya lied, trying to brush past Damu to get into the house. "It's not a good time, bruh."

"This time is better than any." Damu pushed past Malaya and went into her house, but once he got a better look at Malaya and

Anya he grew concerned, seeing them covered in blood. "Where are you hurt, sis?"

"I'm not hurt, Damu.'' Malaya's eyes pleaded Anya for an excuse, a way to explain all of the blood. Damu asked again, "Are you hurt?" Malaya dropped her eyes and shook her head no. "So, where did all the blood come from?"

Not wanting to give any info up to Damu, they both just put their heads down. "Malaya, I just saw my brother and I promised him I would watch over you and protect you. If something would ever happen to you on my watch, he would have me killed. There's no doubt in my mind about that, and that's my brother. That is how much that nigga loves you. Now tell me what the fuck is going on."

Malaya hesitated. "It's Keisha's blood."

"What? Why?" Damu asked, looking confused.

"She had me raped and my daughter killed," Anya spoke up.

"Damn!" Damu said to himself, remembering the beautiful smile A'idah always had on her face when he saw her. "Listen, sit down and explain to me what happened from the beginning."

When Anya and Malaya finished explaining to Damu what had taken place from the beginning up until now, he was mind blown.

"Damn, I respect your gangsta," he said, pulling a Backwoods cigar out of his pocket. "Do you mind, sis? I need one after hearing all the drama that's been going on."

"Go ahead, bruh, and do you."

"Anyone see you when you fucked Keisha over?"

"No. We don't think so."

"Where do you got the rental car parked?"

"In a parking lot near here."

"Well, in the morning we are going to go get the car, have it cleaned inside and out, and then we are going to take it to the car rental. After that, we are not going to mention anything to anybody about this, not even my brother, the less stress the better for him. What was done tonight is supposed to go to the grave with you. Do y'all understand?" Malaya and Anya both nodded their heads up and down in agreement. Damu was going to put his brutha on point

about what happened eventually, but he needed to build Malaya and Anya's trust so he could get to Mike.

CHAPTER 22

CYCLOPS

"OMG! Mrs. Timmons. I'm soooooo sorry!" Hearing Malaya's outburst made Anya think Malaya was going to confess to Mrs. Timmons about what they did to her daughter.

"Don't be sorry, baby. I know Keisha was out there living in those streets. This is truly Allah's creed that she is here. I just wish I could have done more to save her. Come with me. Though she is away, she will be happy to know that you came to see her."

Malaya and Anya entered Keisha's room at Tampa General, not really wanting to be there, but they had to be there to play their part to avoid any suspicion. Once Malaya walked into the hospital room, seeing her once beloved friend in such a grave state, she sought refuge from Allah. *Oh, Allah, forgive us.*

Keisha laid in her hospital bed in a coma, with her face covered in bandages and tubes running from every orifice. Keisha's mother contacted Malaya, telling her that someone attacked her daughter and that she was in critical condition. She wasn't expected to pull through her injuries.

"I know she looks bad," said Mrs. Timmons.

"I'm sorry this happened," Anya said, hugging Keisha's mother, while playing her role. Malaya was fucked up by the sight of Keisha lying in the bed, just a few feet away from her.

"As a mother, I failed my daughter. I was willfully blind to my daughter's actions and deeds." She walked over to her daughter's bedside and rubbed her hand. "The doctors said they had to remove one of her eyes and they had to put three hundred stitches in my baby's face. She suffered broken bones to her legs and to her arm." Mrs.Timmons began to cry. "I don't understand who could have done this. The police say they have no clues as to who might have done this, but I can tell you that the damage done to my baby's face is the work of a woman scorned. Keisha had to be messing around with another woman's husband or boyfriend."

"Did Keisha say—" Malaya was cut off as a tall, slim, dark-skinned girl walked in the room, followed by Mike.

"Hey, Auntie. We are back from picking up the food we ordered," the tall girl said.

"Okay, baby. Thank you so much. You can put my order down over there on the table. Malaya, Anya, this is Keisha's cousin, Iris. She was on the phone with Keisha when she was attacked."

"Hey Iris, did Keisha say anything while she was on the phone with you?" Anya inquired.

"No, she just said she was coming from the Spa of Goddess and walking to her car. Then she yelled out, and then the phone went dead. I called the police and told them what happened, and they went out to the spa and found Keisha in the parking lot." Iris began to cry. "I can't believe this happened to her." Mrs. Timmons rushed over to comfort Iris.

"Oh, this is Mike," Mrs. Timmons said. "He is another one of my daughter's friends."

"I have met the lovely Malaya before, but I don't think I've had the chance to meet Anya,'' Mike said as he extended his hand to Anya. She reluctantly accepted it.

"Hi, Mike. Nice to meet you, but not under the circumstances though." Seeing Mike for the first time made Anya's skin crawl. Many thoughts ran through her mind, just thinking about what she wanted to do with him. It was his madness that caused all the bull-shit. Malaya felt uncomfortable being in Mike's presence, considering the last time she saw him, he was blowing her back out at Keisha's house.

"Mrs. Timmons, I have to go now, but we will be back tomorrow," Malaya said, kissing Mrs. Timmons on the cheek.

"Okay, baby, you be careful out there. As Salaamu Alaikum."

"I will walk them to their car to make sure they get there safely," Mike said, jumping at the opportunity to talk to Malaya. Not wanting to make a scene, Malaya complied. Neither one of them said a word to each other, until they got to the elevator. "I've been calling you, Lay-Lay. Why have you been avoiding me?"

Malaya was getting ready to scream on Mike's ass about him and Keisha running a train on her but catching Anya's eyes let her know she had to put her emotions in check. Shit, after all the pussy was gone already, and she could never get that back.

"I haven't been fucking with you because you haven't been fucking with me. Shit, I have things I need to do and to do them, it takes money."

"Lay-Lay, I can't have you out here like that. I don't know what's going on. Niggas robbed your house, then a few weeks ago Keisha tells me someone broke into her house and trashed her place. I had to replace all her shit. I don't know who's behind all of this."

"Look, Mike. The robbery that happened at my house was probably some random shit, some junkie-ass crackhead gone mad to get high. I need money, and I know Keisha was your runner. All I'm asking is for you to let me and my girl, Anya, run for you. With both of us, that's double the product and double the profit," Malaya said, trying to sell herself and seal the deal. Mike took a deep breath, knowing that without Keisha, his business was going to suffer until he could find someone to replace her, which was no easy task.

"Okay, Lay-Lay. I'm going to give you and your girl a try, but if you fuck this up, I will cut you off." Deep down, Mike felt like the deal was meant to be. He didn't have anyone else lined up to make the trips to Texas and back. Keisha was his ace in the hole.

As Mike reached Malaya's car, he asked, "Do we need to talk about what happened at Keisha's house?"

"No. For what? You did enjoy it right?" Malaya asked, looking into Mike's eyes for any signs that he was sorry.

"Naw, I liked it, but—"

"But what?" Malaya asked as she gave Mike a passionate kiss on his lips and jumped into her car and pulled off.

After seeing the kiss, Anya asked, "What was that all about?"

"It's about using what I got to get what I need. It's time to bring my king home."

Jibril Williams

CHAPTER 23

CAREER MOVE

The last two and a half months were a blur for Malaya and Anya. Not only had Mike let them run his shipment of drugs from Texas to Florida, but he dropped his whole operation in their hands, while he expanded his drug operation from Tampa to St. Pete. All I had been doing was playing puppet master from St. Pete. He called every once in a while, to make sure things were running smoothly in Tampa, or to set a time and date to pick up his money from Malaya and Anya.

Mike's drug operation was demanding all of Malaya's time. Between trying to maintain her day job and keeping up with Mike's operation, she knew something had to give. She decided to take a leave of absence from her job to focus on making this money to bring Velli home.

"Girl, don't forget we have to drop off the work at Roberts Projects," Anya said, placing her last stack of money into the green duffle bag. Malaya and Anya had been counting money for the past two hours.

"Yeah, I know, and we still go to drop them two bricks off to Gold Mouth over on Nebraska Ave. He's been blowing my phone up for the past two hours. Anya, let's go," Malaya said while grabbing the work off the coffee table, and leaving the house, making sure the house was locked up nice and tight. In the rental car, Anya drove while Malaya rode shotgun. Anya's whole demeanor had changed in the last few months, and she was no longer innocent. It was like this new lifestyle was truly her element, to the point where she had made a few runs also.

But what really made Malaya believe Anya was in it to win it, was when they had a situation on Nebraska Avenue one night. After making a drop to some young hustlers, they pushed up on them, telling Anya and Malaya they couldn't leave the block until they gave them some pussy. Out of nowhere, Anya pulls out a chrome 9mm and lets off two shots in the air. The young hustlers broke

camp and Anya and Malaya made a clean getaway. Ever since then, they never had another problem on the Ave. Malaya asked her where she got the gun from. She told her Muhammad left behind some guns when he got locked up.

CHAPTER 24

KEISHA

Keisha laid in her hospital bed with her head in bandages, and her arm and leg in casts. She was still reeling from the news the doctor gave her. She cursed when it was revealed to her they had to remove her left eye and drill a hole in her skull to release the pressure from her swelling brain. It had been three weeks since she came out of her coma. Keisha asked her mother to promise she wouldn't tell anybody she was out of her coma, and to inform the front desk at the hospital that she was not receiving any visitors.

Mrs. Timmons didn't understand why her daughter wanted this request, but she did whatever Keisha asked her to do, because she didn't want anything to stress her daughter. Keisha's instincts told her that her brutal attack had something to do with the threesome she had with Mike and Malaya. She didn't know if Malaya had Mike had done it to her, but whoever did it was going to pay with their lives.

"Let's go hit up Gold Mouth first. Then we can slide past Robert Projects and drop the rest of the work off," Anya said, pulling away from the house.

"Okay. That sounds good to me."

"Give that nigga Gold Mouth a call and let him know we are on our way."

"The Ave is packed. Damn! Look at all these niggas out here!" Malaya complained.

"Where is that black ass nigga at?"

"There he is, in front of Sharon's Corner store," Anya said, whipping the car in front of the store. Gold Mouth jumped in, and they pulled off.

"What's up, baby girl?" Gold Mouth greeted Malaya.

"Ain't too much, just trying to get my money right." It was obvious Gold Mouth liked Malaya. He was always respectful, as Malaya was always nice to him.

"When are going to get out of this game, Malaya? This life isn't for you, baby girl."

"Pssssh, shit! As soon as I get out of the game, I go in for it, but until then there's two bricks." Gold Mouth grabbed the bag from Malaya and checked the work. "Aight. Here you go," Gold Mouth said, handing Malaya two brown paper bags full of money. "You can let me out right here," he instructed Anya. Without hesitation, Anya pulled over and let Gold Mouth out.

"Oh, Malaya. What do you want out of the game? Maybe a nigga like me can give it to you."

With a smile, Malaya looked at Gold Mouth and said, "Velli." Anya pulled off, leaving Gold Mouth looking confused

Pulling up in the Robert Projects, the drug activity was massive. Niggas were crawling through the projects like roaches. Anya likes going there more than any other place the drop work off at, because Malaya told her this was where she first met Redz and he hustles off those projects. That was all Anya needed to hear. She was making two or three trips there a day, trying to get a chance to see Redz again, but she hadn't seen Redz since that night at the mall parking lot with Keisha.

Grabbing the two duffle bags out the backseat, Anya and Malaya made their way to the door of the chop shop. Malaya grabbed her phone and called Biggz, letting him know she was outside the door with the work. This was something Mike had stressed to her always before she showed up at the door. Biggz opened the door, still holding the assault rifle.

"Hey, Malaya! I see that you brought my favorite gangsta girl, Biggz said, eyeing Anya's big ass as she walked through the door, slinging her assets from side to side. Anya hadn't worn a hijab in quite some time.

"Hey, Biggz."Anya smiled.

"Can a big nigga like me get a hug?" he said, smiling at Anya and eyeing her up and down.

"All these naked women around you all day and you want a hug from me?"

"Yeah, baby, they don't have what you have."

"And what's that?"

"Class…" Anya burst out laughing as she gave Biggz a hug.

"Here, Biggz. See to it this work can get out of here," Malaya said, interrupting Biggz and Anya's embrace.

"Okay, you both be careful out there in these streets, but I know you both will be fine, since Anya likes to bust that iron!"

"What-?" Malaya questioned.

"Yeah, I heard about your girl busting her shit," Biggz said with a smile, eyeing the hood's new gangsta girl.

"Oh, Biggz, whatever happened to Redz? I haven't seen him in a while," Malaya said, stopping at the door.

"Oh, that nigga is in St. Pete, playing bodyguard for that nigga, Mike."

"Okay," Malaya said, walking out the door.

"Be safe," Anya said to Biggz, kissing him on the cheek, and not because she liked him, but because of the info he'd just given up on Redz.

Jibril Williams

CHAPTER 25

REJECTED

Anya's palms become sweaty as Muhammad walked in the visiting room. She hadn't seen him in so long, so she didn't know what to expect from her husband. All she knew was she loved him, but the death of their daughter had pushed her to the point of no return.

"As Salaam Alaikum!" Muhammad greeted his wife.

"Wa Alaikum As Salaam." Anya embraced her husband, but his embrace wasn't comforting, nor did she feel any love from his touch. When she went to his lips, Muhammad turned his head, and her kiss was met by his cheek. This small gesture crushed her.

"Please sit and tell me what happened to my daughter, Anya." Looking into Muhammad's eyes, she could see nothing but pure hate. She couldn't tell if his hate was for her or for the person who caused the death of their daughter.

"A'idah died in a home invasion." Thinking back to that day, brought tears to her eyes.

"Why would someone want to rob Malaya's house and kill our daughter?"

"I don't know why, Muhammad, it just happened."

"Was you fucking—fucking with someone out there?"

"Hell no! What type of question you asking me, Muhammad?"

"I just want to know if our daughter's death has anything to do with you out there being foolish."

"I wasn't out there doing anything I wasn't supposed to be doing."

"What about Malaya? Was she involved with anything?" Anya couldn't bring herself to tell her husband Malaya's actions got their daughter killed.

"No, Malaya wasn't into nothing, it just happened, baby."

"I heard you was raped. Is this true?"

"Yes, I was raped." The flood gates opened as the tears began to flow. "Muhammad, how did you know I was raped?"

"Keisha told her little cousin, Iris, and she told me." Hearing this made Anya feel less sorry for doing what she did to Keisha.

"Why did you stay away from me so long?"

"Muhammad, I just needed time to heal and face you. We just lost our child."

Muhammad's jaw tensed as he prepared to give Anya her final rites. "Listen to me, Anya. I think it's best that you leave. I have no need for you anymore. You have been raped, and now you are tainted goods. I could never enter you again. But most of all, you was supposed to be out there taking care of our daughter, but you let her die. Our marriage died when that little girl died. I want a divorce, Anya. I don't want nothing else to do with you."

Pure rage vented through Anya. She blacked out, and hauled off and punched Muhammad with such force, blood shot from his mouth. The contact from Anya's hand to Muhammad's face brought the visiting room to a standstill.

"You motherfucker! After all the shit I've been through with your ass, you're going to abandon me when I need you the most?" Anya yelled at Muhammad. "Now you're talking about tainted goods? Bitch, fuck your ass!" The guards started making their way over to Muhammad and Anya, just relishing in the scene that was unfolding. Anya didn't care. She was going for broke as she hocked a glob of spit in Muhammad's face, and followed it with a close right hook, knocking Muhammad out of his chair. "Fuck you! I hope you rot in this bitch!" By now the guards were grabbing Anya and escorting her out the visiting room.

Breaking down in the car, Anya couldn't believe what just happened. "How could Muhammad just give up on me so damn quickly? Shit! I mean, I held his ass down when he was trying to get ahead in the game. Now he's going to blame me for our daughter's death and talk about I'm tainted goods! My mother told me Muhammad wasn't the man for me and now I wish I never married a man ten years older than me. I wish I would have listened to my mother. Now I'm childless, husbandless, and suffering from a broken heart and a broken spirit," Anya said to herself as she pulled out of the visitation parking lot.

CHAPTER 26

TAINTED GOODS

Walking into Malaya's house, Anya was greeted by Damu.

"What's up, Anya?"

"Everything and nothing," she replied. After hearing Anya's response, Damu went to her.

"Are you alright?" He could tell she had been crying. Damu was taken aback by how much she looked like his ex-wife.

"I'm fine, Damu. Where is Malaya?"

"She's out getting her nails and shit done." He grabbed Anya by the arm. "Please tell me what's wrong. I can tell you've been crying." Unable to hold back her emotions, Anya fell into Damu's arms, breaking down into a fit of tears. She replayed her meeting with Muhammad. Damu couldn't believe his ears.

"You know, Anya, some niggas don't know how to accept certain shit. Some run away and some push away. In your case, Muhammad is pushing away. That's probably the only way he knows how to deal with hesitation."

"Don't care what that man has to deal with or can't deal with. I'm his wife. He is supposed to find a way to deal with it. You don't see Velli acting like a bitch, pushing his wife away, talking about she is tainted goods."

"I know, Anya, but Velli is a different type of nigga."

"Well, I need a different type of nigga right now."

"You don't mean that. Anya, you're just mad right now."

"Shit, Yes, I do. If he don't want me, then I don't want him. I could never forgive Muhammad, Damu."

"I hear ya, but you have to make sure you are not making the wrong decision," Damu said, while releasing Anya from his arms. He relit the half-smoked Backwoods lying in the ashtray.

"Let me hit that," Anya said as she walked over to where Damu was standing, with the burning Kush in his hand. She took the weed from him and took two long pulls. The sweet tasting Kush invaded her lungs. Closing her eyes and letting the Kush take over, Anya

was instantly relaxed. She exhaled. "This some good shit. Do you have any more?" Damu didn't say anything, he just stared at her with a smirk on his face.

"Go ahead and smoke the rest of that. You need it more than I do. You had a rough day today and plus, I got plenty more."

"Thanks, Damu."

Anya wanted to escape from her day. She took another long pull on the Kush and let the smoke out through her nose. Just watching her, Damu knew she must have smoked weed before. Anya was not even conscious of the fact that Damu was watching her, as she walked over to his bottle of Patron 1800 sitting on the table and took a sip from the bottle.

"Whoa! Hold up, Anya. You're moving too fast."

"Damu, I got this. I just need a little something to relax my nerves."

"Okay, just take it easy. That's some strong shit you're sipping on. Have you found out anything about that nigga Redz?"

"Yeah, I heard from Biggz that he's out in St. Pete, playing bodyguard for Mike," Anya replied, taking another pull from the kish. "The first chance I get, I'm going to murder that nigga for what he did to my daughter."

"I hear you, Anya, but that's a big boy game you trying to play when you talking about murder. Are you sure you are ready for that?"

With eyes glazed over, Anya stared straight into Damu. "Yeah, I'm more ready than I'll ever be."

"I see you got your mind made up but let me help you with this. I know what I'm doing, and what it takes to pull something like this off. You just roll up on Redz and shoot him… if you do that, you are going to jail for the rest of your life. That would be a false move."

"I don't have anything else to live for, Damu. Everything has been taken away from me." Amya started to cry.

"You have everything to live for. You just have to find out what's important to you, Anya."

"I can't think right now, Damu. I'm going to take a shower."

"Okay. I'm going to be right here," Damu said as he watched Anya walk towards the bathroom. He still can't believe how much she looked like his beloved wife. Damu was thinking about how much he misses her. "Allah, why did you have to take her away from me?" Damu whispered to himself.

Anya stripped down to her panties and bra, thumping the last of the weed she was smoking into the toilet. She had a nice buzz going on. Turning the shower on and adjusting the hot water to her liking, she unhooked her bra and stepped out her panties. She stepped into the shower and the hot water brought her body to life. Anya stood under the shower for a few minutes, letting the soothing water run over her body. The even set of the day started to fade away. Grabbing the Victoria's Secret body wash from the shelf, she began to lather her body down.

She still couldn't seem to wrap her mind around the fact that Muhammad could kick her to the curb, after all they had been through together. *Tainted goods. How fuckin' dare he say that shit to me? My goods are not spoiled. If my heart is good, then everything else is good*, she thought as she rubbed the body wash between her legs, cleaning her love box. On contact, her clit lit up like a light bulb. Stroking her hands back and forth over her clit, Anya let out a moan. "Mmmmmmmmmmmm." She bit down on her bottom lip.

"How the fuck could he ever think my pussy is tainted?" She thought about Muhammad's cruel words. "Shit, no man in their right mind would ever think I'm not good. Anya stroked harder. "Nobody would ever think that. Nobody, not Biggz. Not Damu."

Just mentioning Damu's name made her open her eyes. "I'm here in the shower playing with my pussy. If my husband doesn't want me, then there's no reason for me to continue to be faithful to him," Anya said as she turned the water off and stepped out of the shower. The alcohol and the Kush were working to full effect. Anya walked out the bathroom and into the living room, where Damu was still sitting, thinking about his wife. He was so deep in thought, he didn't see Anya approaching him butt naked.

"Damu, hold me."

"What do you say, Anya?" Damu questioned while snapping out of his daze and turning his head towards her. Seeing her standing there in her birthday suit, caused him to spill his drink in his lap.

"I said, hold me."

"Please, Anya, put your clothes on. I—"

"I don't need for you to feel sorry for me, Damu. I need you to hold me. I need to be touched. It's been so long, Damu."

Damu stood and embraced Anya. She didn't waste my time as she placed soft kisses on his lips. He accepted her tongue as his manhood started to grow in his pants. Slowly, his hands started to explore her body, starting with her round, soft ass. Anya gasped for air and stuck her tongue deeper into Damu's mouth. When Damu took a firm grip of her with his hands, Anya's hands worked fast, unbuckling Damu's pants and releasing his eight-inch love stick. Anya let his pants drop around his ankles to get a better feel of the thick head of Damu's manhood. His erection grazed her stomach, making her break their kiss for a second, in order to get Damu's shirt over his head.

Damu kicked his shoes off and stepped out of his pants. Damu played Anya on the couch and got between her legs, working his way between her thighs. He didn't waste any more time. He had to taste the woman that looked so much like his dearly departed wife. He plunged his face into her box, tasting her sweet nectar. Shock waves of pleasure shot through her body. Anya grabbed the back of Damu's head and pulled his face deeper into her pussy. Damu didn't mind. He ate her from the bottom out.

"Oh, Da-Damu. Please, don't stop. I'm about to cum... please... Oh please, Damu!" She let off a helluva scream, "Aaaaw-wwww!" as she came inside of Damu's mouth.

Sucking the lips of her love box clean, Damu leveled himself over her and asked, "Are you sure you want this, Anya?"

"Damu, please give it to me," Anya pleaded.

"There's no turning back, if we go there."

"We have already gone too far. Why stop now? I want you, Damu."

That was all Damu needed to hear. He opened Anya's legs wide, and grabbed the tip of his manhood. He parted the lips of her love box and slowly pushed the head inside of her.

"Ohhhhhhh!" Anya moaned.

"What the fuck is going on in here?" Malaya shouted as she walked in her house, catching her best friend and her husband's brother fucking on her couch.

Jibril Williams

CHAPTER 27

GRAVESITE

Malaya couldn't comprehend what was transpiring in front of her eyes. Never in a thousand years did she ever think she would catch her best friend and brother-in-law fucking in her home, on her couch.

"Oh, shit!" Damu said as he jumped off Anya's naked body, grabbing his clothes off the floor and making a break for the bathroom. Anya wasted no time getting back into her clothes, embarrassment was written all over her face.

"Anya, what the hell are you doing? Have you lost your damn mind?"

"No, I haven't lost my mind. I just lost my heart and Shaytan got the best of me."

"What are you talking about, girl?" Malaya asked as the tears rolled down Anya's face.

"Malaya, please. I don't want to talk about it right this minute. I'm not ready to relive what I went through today."

"I thought you went to go see Muhammad today."

"I did, and it was all bad."

"Was it bad enough for you to leave there and come here and fuck Damu?" Rolling her eyes, Malaya was getting annoyed with her at the same time.

"Look, I'm a grown ass woman, and like I said, I don't want to talk about it right now. I'll be back through here tomorrow to help you make them drops. Right now, I have to clear my head."

Anya's demeanor had Malaya looking at her sideways. "Aight then. I guess I'll see you tomorrow, but know that we are sisters and no matter what you are going through, I'm here for you. Always."

"Thanks, Malaya. I needed to hear that." She hugged her best friend and walked out the door.

"Damu! Bring that ass out of the bathroom! Somebody is going to tell me what the hell is going on!"

"What's up, sis?" Damu said casually while coming out of the bathroom, drying his hands. "Before you go off on me, I'm sorry you caught me out of pocket like that in your house, but it's hard to explain what I'm feeling for your girl right now. Especially when I'm around her, it's something I just can't explain."

"What! Damu, you talking crazy. You know Anya is married, right?"

"Yeah, to a man who no longer wants her. She's married to a man that views her as tainted goods."

"Tainted goods?" Malaya repeated, frowning her face up like something stinks. "Damu, who told you that? Muhammad worships the ground Anya walks on."

"Well, apparently he don't anymore."

"Damu, tell me what happened. What's going on?"

"I think it's best you talk to Anya about that. She will tell you everything in due time."

"Yeah, bro, you're right. When she is ready, we'll talk."

***

Anya stood at the foot of her daughter's grave. "My loving daughter, how are you doing today? I know you miss Mommy, and Mommy misses you too. I went to see your daddy today and things didn't go too well. He is frustrated that you are no longer here with us on Earth." The tears started flowing from her eyes as she thought about the past events that led up to her standing at the foot of her daughter's grave.

"Ummi, please don't worry. I don't like it when you cry, Mommy."

"I know you don't like it when Mommy cries, but I just miss you so much, A'idah."

"Did the bad man with a gun hurt you, Mommy?" A'idah asked with a sad voice.

"Yes, the bad man with the gun hurt me because he took you away from me. I hate him for that, A'idah. I really do, baby girl."

"You told me never to hate, Mommy."

"I know. I just can't help it, A'idah. Some things you just can't help feeling. But you know that?"

"What, Ummi?"

"I'm going to hurt that bad man. I'm going to send him to a place where he'll never hurt anybody else. Then I'm going to come where you are, and we'll never be apart again. There's nothing here for me on this Earth."

"What about Daddy, Mommy? He's there on Earth, right Mommy?"

"Daddy will be happier if you and I are together. Then I can take better care of you."

"Okay, Mommy. I can't wait for the day to come, so we can play together, and you can read to me like you used to do before I go to bed."

"It won't be long, baby girl. It won't be long, I promise," Anya said as she knelt down and kissed her daughter's headstone.

Jibril Williams

CHAPTER 28

GOVERNMENT'S DECEIT

Malaya rolled over in frustration as her cell phone rang nonstop. Seeing it was 7:30 in the morning, she was thinking about ignoring the call, but the familiar looking number indicated the caller was calling from Washington, DC. Automatically, Malaya knew whoever was calling, it was pertaining to her husband.

"Hello," Malaya answered in her sleepy voice.

"Good morning. This is Velli's lawyer, Mr. McCullough." Hearing Velli's lawyer on the phone, Malaya sat straight up and rubbed the cold out of her sleepy eyes, hoping it was some good news about her husband's case.

"Hey, Mr. McCullough."

"Hey, Malaya. I have been trying to contact you for a week now, but you haven't been answering your phone."

"I'm sorry, I've been very busy. I take it you got the money that I sent to your office?"

"Yes, I did receive the check and I've already given the DNA analyzer his share to start processing the unprocessed DNA evidence taken from the crime scene. The results may take a few weeks or months for them to come back, but until then, I will be working on other avenues in your husband's case."

"Mr. McCullough, what type of DNA was found at my husband's scene?"

"Well, since you asked, there were boot prints, fingerprints and saliva found. The fingerprints were on the victim's car, and the boot prints were found around the victim's car, where he was shot. But that's not the most fascinating part, Mrs. Williams. There were two different types of bullets found in the victim's skull."

"What! What do you mean there were two different types of bullets found at the crime scene?"

"No, not two different bullets found at the crime scene, but in the victim's body..." Malaya's heart dropped. She couldn't believe what she was hearing.

"Mr. McCullough, are you telling me that we are talking about two shooters?"

"Yes! That's exactly what I'm saying to you."

"But why didn't this ever come up in trial?"

"I think the government wants your husband so badly, they did whatever they needed to do to get him. They withheld evidence or should we say, they did not process all the evidence in the case. I think once they got the tip your husband was the possible shooter in the case, the police went to search Velli's house and found that 9mm handgun. They thought they had their man off the break and did not process the evidence that was at the crime scene, trying to save money for the government.

"The shell casings did not match the 9mm gun found at Velli's house. Nor were the boots on Velli's feet compared to the prints found at the crime scene. So, if we can prove that Velli's fingerprints don't match and the other DNA does not link Velli to the crime, I think we have a great chance of your husband walking free. But Mrs. Williams, this will take some more time and more money."

"Okay, Mr. McCullough. Just get my husband home. I will get you your money." Hearing Malaya say that brought a smile to his face.

"Well, Mrs. Williams, I must go. I have a meeting with a client in twenty minutes."

"Okay, Mr. McCullough. That sounds like a plan to me, and please, as soon as you get the results back, give me a call."

"I most definitely will, Mrs. Williams." Mr. McCullough said as he disconnected the call. Malaya was so excited from the news she just received, she felt like everything she'd been through wasn't in vain. Her plan was slowly starting to come together. Soon, her husband would be in her arms again. That thought alone made her feel like she was on top of the world.

CHAPTER 29

CAUGHT SLIPPIN'

Mike and his three goons sat in the corner booth of the sports bar downtown St. Pete, watching the Washington Redskins and Miami Dolphins game.

"Damn, them Dolphins can't score shit on them 'Skins," Money Roy cried, because he knew by the end of the night, he would be paying Redz two grand for a bet they placed on the game.

"You should have known not to bet that money on them Dolphins! Their defense can't handle the Redskins' offense," Redz replied, aggravating Money Roy even further.

"You silly ass niggas sitting around betting on other niggas that's already getting millions," Mike taunted. "Them niggas out there on the field got theirs. They got them fly ass whips, them big ass houses and they fucking some of the baddest bitches you have ever seen. While you niggas sitting here, betting your money on some muthafuckas that don't even know you exist.

"Shit, them muthafuckas out on tha field already winning. Even if they lose a game, them niggas are paid out their ass, but we still trying to get where they are. And we will never be them millionaire motherfuckers out on that field, unless we step our game up and take this damn city over!" Mike made his intentions clear.

"Boss man, we got that shit," Redz said while downing his drink. "We got most of the city on lock. All we have to do now is drop that nigga, Lil L, then everything is all ours and it is smooth sailing from there."

"See, that's the shit I'm talking about. Most is not good enough. We need the whole damn city right now! Are you content with just working for free? You niggas could run your own city. You got to think big, nigga, and stop thinking small. The reason why we haven't smashed that nigga Lil L is because he is still hungry."

"Man, fuck Lil L," Mike's goon with the dirty dreadlocks and golds in his mouth said.

"I'm going to put so many holes in that nigga when I catch him."

"Well, I tell you what. I got a half a mil ticket on that nigga's head. I'll see if that'll get you niggaz back hungry."

Mike looked at his goons so see what type of reaction this would bring. The mention of half a mil made all the men stop talking.

"Man, that's half a mil," Dread Head said out loud. Redz knew Mike was worth a few millions, hands down, but would he really be willing to give up a half a million to have just one nigga murked? In that case, the city of St. Pete must be worth more to him than he led them to believe.

"I'm in," Redz replied.

"Count me in too, boss man," the rest of the goons joined in.

"Well, let's get it done," Mike said as he pushed out of the booth. The rest of his goons downed their drinks and followed the boss out of the bar. Once outside, the cool Florida air hit them while they were walking towards their truck. Mike did not see the two gunmen six cars away, ducking down between the cars in the parking lot, with AK-47's in their hands.

They had been out there for the last two hours, waiting for Mike and his goons to come out of the sports bar. One of the waitresses working the sports bar saw Mike and his people come in earlier, and she immediately placed a call to Lil L.

Redz's phone vibrated in his pocket. Pulling it out, he saw that it was Keisha, texting him, saying she needed some alone time with him. Redz smiled because even though Keisha's face was cut up, her pussy was well intact, and he was planning on getting some tonight. *No cuddling will be going on*, he thought as he started to return Keisha's text. His phone slipped out from his hand and hit the ground.

"Shit, I hope I didn't break my fucking phone," Redz said as he bent down to grab his phone from the ground. He saw two figures creeping with their guns in their hands. Redz yelled out, "It's a hit! Get the fuck down!" as he reached for his gun at his waist.

The parking lot lit up like the Fourth of July. *Yak-Yak-Yak-Yak-Yak-Yak-Boom-Boom-Boom-Boom.*

Mike's goons were strapped too, but their guns were no match for the assault rifles. Money Roy's chest was opened up, exposing his insides. The contact from the AK-47 flipped Dread Head so quickly, he didn't even get a chance to pull his gun. Mike and Redz returned fire, dropping one of the gunmen. Hearing the sirens in the distance, the gunmen fled and Mike and Redz jumped in the truck and made their getaway.

"Fuck!" Mike yelled, beating on the steering wheel. "That was that nigga, Lil L's work! Find that nigga and murk his ass!"

Jibril Williams

CHAPTER 30

DAMU'S VISIT

Inmate Machiavelli Williams, number 07085-007," the C.O. yelled from the office door. Hearing this broke Velli's concentration from his next move he was going to make on the chess board.
"Yeah, C.O.!" Velli yelled back.
"Report to visitation. You have a visit."
"Aight," Velli said as he pushed away from the chess table. "It's my move when I get back," Velli told his old timer, Joe James.
"Have a good one, young blood."
"Yeah. Thanks, slim."
"Who is coming to see you? I thought your wife was coming to see you tomorrow?" the old head said as he stood up in front of the table and stretched his legs that had become stiff from sitting at the table too long.
"I don't know who this is, old head. It still might be the wife. You know, she is missing me so much, she might have decided to come a day early." Velli smiled. "Let me get to the visiting room. I'll see you later."
"Bet, young blood. Later!"
Velli was feeling good, especially since he received a letter from Mr. McCullough, stating he received the money from his wife on his behalf to have some unprocessed evidence processed. If things went in his favor, he would be seeing some daylight soon, and he could get his wife out of the mess she got herself into, even though it was for his sake. He worried about Malaya and Anya often. Many nights he couldn't sleep, thinking about them. He never lost a child before, but he admired Anya's strength to keep moving, especially after Muhammad told her he was divorcing her. How could Muhammad do that to her after all they had been through? This plagued and puzzled Velli.
Velli shook his head just thinking about what she might be going through mentally, but his thoughts were shrouded in guilt, knowing his wife's actions could have led to the death of A'idah.

"Oh, Allah, forgive us." Walking into the visiting room, Velli scanned the room looking for his wife, but seeing Damu brought a big smile to his face.

"Salaam, (peace) big bruh. Damn, you getting big, what they feeding you in there?" Damu teased.

"Salaam, Damu." Velli smiled as he hugged his little brother. "Man, it's good seeing you, little bro."

"And it's even better seeing you. I see you are in better spirits than the last time I saw you."

"Yeah, that's because I have some good news and the hope at the end of the tunnel just got a little brighter, but it's nothing to start singing about."

"So, what is it?" Damu got hyped, just thinking about his brother having another chance of walking the streets sometime soon.

"Well, I'm not going into details, but the lawyer found some new evidence in the case that might set me off. Right now, they're having the new evidence sent to the lab to be analyzed. But, we will see what happens in a few weeks or the next few months."

"Damn, bruh, you're getting ready to shine."

"Insha Allah, I will if Allah sees fit. But tell me, did you get on that business for me?"

"Yeah and no, slim."

"What do you mean, Damu?" Velli's demeanor became serious.

"I'm on top of it, but that nigga Mike been MIA. He got Malaya and Anya running his whole operation in Tampa. I got word from Anya that he's in St. Pete, trying to expand his business."

Velli put his head in his hands and just listened. "Fuck! You telling me that nigga got my wife out there that deep in the game? I bet that nigga is taking cold advantage of her and Anya, paying them trick money while he's taking eighty-five percent of the profits. Damu, I want that nigga murked. Fuck the money. Murk his ass the first chance you get."

"Hold up, bruh. We had a plan. Let's stick with it. I think I can pull this off once I get a good line on this nigga."

"Naw, Damu—"

"Bruh you always taught me not to make decisions out of anger. I know that you are angry, but chill. I got this. I know how to murk a nigga when the time is right."

"Man, you don't know how it feels being in here, and my wife's out here going through shit. I feel like my hands are tied. I feel helpless."

"I know what you feel, Velli, I do. Just let me handle this out here and you just stay on the lawyer's ass. Malaya can take care of herself. She's a big girl," Damu said, thinking about the night he caught her and Anya covered in Keisha's blood.

"Okay, Damu, I'll try to chill. Just promise me you will handle that order for me."

"I promise, bruh. I'll take care of it."

Jibril Williams

CHAPTER 31

MOVING ON

"Malaya, get that ass up, girl. We got shit to do today," Anya yelled from the kitchen. Malaya was out of bed, exhausted from all the rippin' and runnin' they did last night. It seemed like every hustler on Nebraska Avenue wanted to buy work last night. They didn't get in the house until 4:00 that morning, and Anya was already cooking breakfast and it was just 9:30 a.m.

After going the bathroom taking her morning pee and brushing her teeth, Malaya made her way to the kitchen, where she was met with the aroma of fried turkey bacon and scrambled eggs. Malaya walked into the kitchen to find her road dawg over the stove with some pink booty shorts on and a wife beater, smoking a tightly rolled Backwoods stuffed with Kush.

"Girl, put some damn clothes on and that weed out while you are cooking my food."

"Oh. Hey, girl," Anya said, ignoring Malaya's demands to put the weed out and put some clothes on. Anya had been smoking weed ever since that day she came from seeing Muhammad and he told her he wanted a divorce.

"How do you want your eggs? Scrambled or fried hard?"

"Scrambled please," Malaya said as she made her way to the fridge to get some orange juice. Grabbing a glass from the clean dish rack, Malaya turned towards the kitchen table, only to be greeted by Anya's chrome 45 sitting on the table.

"Anya, why you got that gun sitting out on my table?"

Looking over her shoulder from the stove, Anya giggled. "Girl, I don't know. I just feel more comfortable when I have my baby around."

"Your baby?"

"Yeah. My baby never lets me down," Anya said with a smile.

Malaya just shook her head and drank her orange juice. The ringtone of Nikki Minaj's song, "I Did It On Them" invaded the quietness of the kitchen. "Hey, Damu. Yeah, I got your breakfast,"

Anya laughed into the phone. "Yeah, come and get it while it's hot," she said in her sexy voice. "You're out front? Aight, come on in. Malaya, would you please let Damu in? He brought raisin bread for our breakfast." Rolling her eyes, Malaya went to open the door for her brother-in-law.

"Hey, Damu."

"What's up, sis?" Damu stood there with a grin on his face. "Damn, it smells good in here. Whatchu cooking?"

"That's Anya in there with her gangsta boo ass." Damu laughed as he was pushed by Malaya and went straight to the kitchen with a loaf of raisin bread swinging in his hand.

"Hey gorgeous!" Damu said as he walked in the kitchen, eyed Anya at the stove cooking in those booty shorts, exposing the bottom of her caramel-colored ass cheeks.

"Hey, Damu." Anya ran and jumped in Damu's arms, wrapping her arms around his neck and her thick legs around his waist, placing sloppy kisses on his cheeks. Malaya just stared at their display of public affection with her mouth wide open.

"Wow, somebody's happy to see me," Damu said while putting Anya in a bear hug, fighting the urge to grab a handful of her ass. Anya and Damu had grown close ever since he put that mean head game down on her that day when Muhammad rejected her. When she wasn't making money with Malaya, she was with Damu.

"What are you cooking, woman?" Damu said, placing Anya back on her feet.

"Just some turkey bacon and scrambled eggs. I know you have to be at the shop, so I made you a plate. It's in the microwave."

"Thanks, babe!" He went over to the microwave to check out the contents were on his plate. "Mmmmm! This looks so good, Anya. I'm sorry I can't sit down and enjoy this lovely meal with you and Malaya, but I got to open the shop. Jose is there waiting on me. We have seven yards to cut today."

"I see the landscaping biz is doing well."

"Yeah, it pays the bills and keeps me honest."

"Are we still going to the movies tonight, Damu?"

"Yeah, I wouldn't miss that for nothing in the world," Damu said with a smile. "Aight, let me get out of here. You both should be careful out there today."

"Hold up, Damu."

"What's up, Anya?"

"Make sure you take a shower. I don't want to be out with you smelling like grass."

"Oh, you got jokes, huh? We will see just how funny you are tonight." Damu laughed as he walked out the door.

"So, you two are dating now?" Malaya asked, watching her best friend's body language.

"Naw, we're just cool, that's all."

"Just cool? Girl, I caught you fucking on my couch! It seems like you two are more than 'just cool' to me, girl."

"For the record, we didn't fuck on your couch. We were about to fuck, and we have not tried since then."

"Yeah, right," Malaya said, rolling her eyes. "You and Damu are damn near together every day."

"I just enjoy his company, Malaya."

"What happened between you and Muhammad?"

Anya's demeanor changed when she heard Muhammad's name.

"Sis, that ungrateful nigga don't want to be with me."

"What? Why would you say something like that? Muhammad loves everything about you."

"That's bullshit, Malaya. That nigga only loved me because of A'idah."

"That's not true, Anya."

"It's the truth! He told me! Do you know what else that ungrateful motherfucker had the nerve to say to me?" Anya asked in a fit of rage.

Not really wanting to hear any more, Malaya reluctantly asked. "What else did Muhammad say?"

"That faggot had the fucking nerve to tell me he could never enter me again, because I was raped. He called me tainted goods." Anya broke down crying. Malaya rushed over to where Anya was

standing, wrapped her arms around her friend, and they both cried together.

CHAPTER 32

TRUE INTENTIONS

Sliding the tight fitted, all-white True Religion jeans over her voluptuous ass, Anya checked her curves in the mirror. "Damn, I'm so phat!" she said to herself, running her hands over her hips, thighs, and ass. Anya admired her five-foot-nine hourglass frame in the full-length mirror. Her golden complexion and new pixie haircut complimented her dark almond-shaped eyes. Throwing on an all-black, button-down Gucci shirt and matching Gucci slip-ons, she was ready to spend the night with Damu. As she placed the last touches of lip gloss on her lips, Anya walked into Malaya's room.

"Malaya, I'm going to be leaving in a few minutes."

"Alright, damn! Look at you!" Malaya smiled.

"You don't think this too much?" Anya said, putting on her innocent girl performance.

"Naw, sis. You are good. But, for a person you claim to be just cool with and you are just friends with, you sure are going out your way to look sexy for him," Malaya replied with a smirk on her face.

"Whatever. I look sexy even when I'm rocking a hijab." Just the mention of the word "hijab" made both of them remember how far they were from their Islamic path.

Downplaying the statement that was made, Malaya asked, "What movie are you going to see?"

"Hmmmm. I'm not sure, sis," Anya said, picking up her phone to call Damu to see where he was.

"See, that's how I know it's more to it than you two being really good friends. You're going to a movie with Damu and you don't even know what movie you're going to see? You just want to be around him, no matter what he's doing or where he's going." Malaya laughed. Anya gave her the finger and began talking on the phone.

"Hey, ba... hey, Damu. Where are you at? Oh, okay. I'm ready." Anya disconnected her call.

"He just pulled up out front. I gotta go, girl. Love you."

"Love you too." Malaya followed behind Anya to the front door.

"I left you a little something on the nightstand to hold you down until I get back. All you have to do is pick it up, point, and squeeze the trigger."

"Okay, Anya. Girl, now go have some fun."

Damu was sitting outside in a red Charger, watching Anya strut towards his car. "Damn! She is stacked! Man, she looks more and more like Crystal every time I see her, especially since she cut her hair," he said to himself. Opening the door to the Charger, Anya was greeted by the sounds of Beyoncé, singing "Dangerously in Love."

"Oh, shit! That's my song!" Anya cried out. "You must be trying to get you some tonight," she teased.

Damu fired back, "Shoot, you already owe me some head!" They both burst out laughing.

Suddenly getting serious, Damu asked, "How are you feeling, beautiful? How have you been holding up?" Anya's heart melted at all the attention Damu gave her.

"I'm blessed, babe, in more ways than you can imagine."

Pulling away from Malaya's house, Damu asked, "What movie do you want to see?" Anya really didn't feel like a movie. She wanted to get to know Damu a little better, and on a different level.

"Hmmmmmmm. I don't really want to see a movie, Damu."

"Okay, what do you really want to do? Where do you want to go?"

"Pull over, let me drive, and I'll show you what I want to do." Damu fulfilled Anya's request. He whipped his car to the curb and exchanged places with Anya. Pulling away from the curb, Anya handled the muscle car like a boss bitch, as she zipped through traffic. Damu leaned his seat back and watched Anya, undressing her with his eyes. He couldn't get over how thick and nicely shaped her thighs were.

"Where are we going, Anya?"

"Just lay back and enjoy the ride. Trust me, where we are going, you won't be disappointed," she said with a smirk on her face.

"Aight, babe, I'm going to hold you to that," Damu said, firing up the Kush he had already rolled. Rolling up on the Grand Hyatt and seeing the hotel, Dam already knew what time it was. After the valet pulled away with the car, Anya didn't waste any time. She grabbed Damu by the hand and escorted him straight through the lobby. The lobby was a blur to Damu. All he was focusing on was Anya's ass as she walked across the lobby floor, heading straight to the elevator.

Seeing that she didn't have to check in at the front desk, Damy knew this was pre-planned. He smiled to himself, knowing Anya wanted him as much as he wanted her. Getting into the elevator, Damu couldn't help himself as he gripped a handful of Anya's ass. Anya pushed back onto him and grinded on his manhood, constantly bringing him to life. The elevator opened on the third floor. Anya grabbed Damu by his erect penis that press against his jeans and walked him down the hall, until he reached room 312.

Anya guided Damu into the room and went straight to work, tonguing him down passionately. She sucked his bottom lip, while stroking his dick. Damu started to unbutton his shirt, but she knocked his hand away.

"Get naked. I've been waiting too long for this," Anya whined while snatching her clothes off and throwing them on the floor. Damu did what he was told. He was naked before Anya was. She wanted to feel Damu inside of her so bad. It had been so long since she'd been penetrated. "Damn you, Muhammad," she cussed under her breath. Anya pushed Damu on the bed and looked into his eyes.

It's time I pay you what I owe you." She wasted no time placing his manhood in her mouth. Damu cried out in pleasure while grabbing the back of Anya's head, guiding her head up and down on his dick. Moments later, she climbed on top of him and eased herself on him. It felt like she was a virgin all over again, she was so tight. It took a moment to get all of Damu's manhood inside of him, but once she did, she had no problem blowing his mind.

Jibril Williams

CHAPTER 33

PICTURES NEVER LIE

"Mail call!" the C.O. yelled out. All the inmates rushed over to the C.O. doing mail calls, hoping their loved ones dropped them a few lines or a card to remind them that they were still loved and missed. "D. Jones, Elliott Wallace, Andre Smith," the C.O. went on, calling names out. "M. Williams!" This broke Velli's concentration from his chess game.

"Who?" Velli called back.

"M. Williams," the C.O. yelled back.

"Which M. Williams?"

"Machiavelli Williams," the C.O. replied.

"That's me. Hold up, old timer, let me grab this mail from the C.O." Velli walked over and grabbed the mail from the C.O., thinking it was something his wife had sent him, but he was thrown off by the no-return address that was in the envelope. What was most confusing was the odd handwriting it belonged to. The envelope had a stamp on it that read, "Photos: Don't Bend."

Who the fuck is this? Velli thought as he walked back over to finish his chess game, stuffing the envelope in his pocket.

***

Anya laid with her head on Damu's chest, tracking the muscles of his six-pack with her fingers.

"Damu, tell me about Crystal?" Anya asked, now placing small kisses on his chest.

"What? How do you know about Crystal?" This topic broke Damu out of his after-sex glow.

"You have her name tattooed on your chest, fool," she giggled.

"Oh, well... Crystal is my wife."

"What! Your wife!" Anya shouted, raising her head off his chest.

"My deceased wife, I mean."

"Oh!" Anya was relieved. "What happened to her, if you don't mind me asking?"

"She was killed a few years ago when I used to live in DC."

"How was she killed?"

"Listen, I don't want to talk about that sadness right now, but I do want you to know what I feel for you is real. I don't want you to think otherwise when I tell you this, and I'm telling you this because of how you make me feel. You mean a lot to me."

"What is it, Damu?"

"You look like my deceased wife."

"Okay, and what does that mean?"

"No, I mean you can go for her twin sister, that's how much you look like her. The only thing different is she was deaf and you're not."

"Hold up. Are you fucking with me because I look like her?"

"Hell no, Anya. I know you two are two different people. I like you for you. I love you for helping me love again."

"Love? You can't love me, Damu. I'm tainted goods."

"There's nothing tainted about you, don't believe that bullshit your husband feeds you."

"Damu, I'm not ready to take on love right now. I just want to get the motherfucker who killed my daughter, and help Malaya get this money together to get Velli out of prison. I have to do these things first, Damu. I respect your heart for loving me, but right now I'm on a mission."

"Okay, Anya. I respect that but let me help. Let's work together. I have something on my plate. It seems your mission is my mission. I told you before, I'll help you with the Redz situation, but I promised Velli I would kill that nigga, Mike after I rob him. I need my brother home and I'm determined to get him on the other side of that penitentiary fence."

"Aight, Damu. Help me get Redz and I'll help you get Mike."

"That's a deal, babe."

"Well, that's a deal," Anya said, as she straddled him and rode him for the third time.

***

"Check," the old head said as he threatened Velli's king with a rook. Velli blocked the check by placing his knight in front of his king.

"Out of check," Velli called. The old head pushed his pawn up to put some protection on his rook. Velli wasn't worried about the move, he had the old head set up for a checkmate. Velli took hold of the old head's pawn that was in front of his king, with his queen. "Checkmate," Velli called out. Velli's bishop was protecting his queen, so the old head couldn't take his queen.

"Damn. Good game, Velli. Want to play another one?"

"Naw, I'm done for the day. I'm about to hit the showers."

Velli shook the old head's hand and made his way to his cell. He put the flap up over the cell window so he could undress to take his shower. As he was pulling off his shoes and pants, the envelope fell out of his pocket. "Oh shit," Velli said to himself. "I forgot I had some mail." Looking at the front of the envelope, he was puzzled as to why there wasn't a return address on the letter. He opened the letter and pulled the contents out. Velli's mind went blank as he stared at the images of Mike and Malaya laying together in bliss.

Jibril Williams

CHAPTER 34

REDZ

"Anya, whatever happened with you and Damu the other night? You stayed MIA for almost two days."

"Girl, you know I'm a big girl, and I don't kiss and tell." Anya grinned at Malaya.

"But, Damu—"

"Malaya, you are nosey as hell, counting the days that I've been gone and shit." Anya burst out laughing.

"Well, you left a bitch here all alone." Malaya threw back. "Oh yeah, and don't think I didn't see Damu palm your ass before he left a few minutes ago."

"Damn, Malaya, you don't miss shit!"

"Well, if you want me to miss something, don't do it in front of me," Malaya teased and stuck her tongue out at Anya.

"Malaya, leave me alone! I don't have time for your mess, I need to take a shower."

"Yeah, make sure you take a cold one, so you can cool your hot ass down some!'' They both burst out laughing as Anya went into the bathroom.

Moments later, Malaya's phone interrupted her laughing with her girl. "Hello?"

"Hey, Damu. Damu, you just left here. You're missing my girl, or should I be saying you're missing your girl already?"

"Ha-ha-ha, you got jokes, sis? Yeah, I miss her, but that's not why I'm calling."

"Okay, what's up then and whose number are you calling me from?"

"I left my cell phone in the kitchen. I've been trying to call Anya to bring it to me. I'm at Brother's Barber Shop, four blocks from where y'all live, off Nebraska Ave. Do you know where that's at?"

"Yeah, bruh. I know where the barber shop is. Anya is in the shower, so I'll run the phone down there to you."

"Aight, sis. See you in a minute."

"Okay, Damu." Malaya disconnected the call.

"Anya! Damu left his phone. I'm going to take it to him. He's at the barber shop on the Ave. I'll be right back."

"Alright," Amya yelled from the shower. "Tell Damu I said hiiiiiii!" Malaya just shook her head, grabbed Damu's phone off the kitchen table and exited the front door. *Damn, it feels good out here*, Malaya thought as she jumped into her car. The Ave was busy as always as Malaya maneuvered through traffic. As she drove past Sharon's Corner store, she saw Gold Mouth out there, running his spot like a real floor general. Things have been going good for her lately. Malaya had a hundred and twenty-five thousand stashed at a storage space Anya didn't even know about.

Anya had been giving Malaya her half of the money she'd been making from working for Mike. Malaya couldn't let herself take all of Anya's money, so once she got the money up to pay Velli's lawyer, Malaya started putting money away. Her plan was for Velli, Damu, Anya and herself to relocate once Velli got outta prison. She wanted to go somewhere far away from all the drama.

Pulling up in front of the barber shop, Malaya hopped out and double parked by a blue Lexis. She ran into the barber shop, while all the guys in front of the barber shop looked at her like she was crazy with her hijab on. She saw Damu paying the barber for cutting his hair, and Malaya walked over to him.

"Hey, bruh! Here's your phone."

"Okay, thanks, sis. I owe you one."

"Let me go. I got my car double parked out front."

"Okay, let me walk you to your car."

"One day you are going to lose that phone and you are never going to get it back."

"Yeah, I know. I gotta do better about keeping up with my phone. I don't know—"

"What's up, Malaya?" Redz interrupted as he stepped towards Malaya with open arms. Damu saw Redz advancing towards Malaya, and he stepped in between Redz and Malaya, putting his hand up to Redz's chest, preventing the embrace with Anya

"Nobody hugs her except her husband and me," Damu spoke up. Sensing the challenge, Redz knocked Damu's hand away.

"Man, get the fuck out my way!" Redz said, getting mad and feeling disrespected.

"Hold up!" Malaya shouted, seeing Damu reaching for his gun. "Redz, this is my husband's brother, Damu. Damu, this is Redz." Damu already knew who he was and what he was all about.

"Oh my bad, slim," Damu said, while stepping in between Malaya and Redz. Redz felt like he'd heard Damu's name before. He looked Damu up and down, but he couldn't seem to place his face.

"So, what's up, Malaya?" Redz was still trying to get that hug from Malaya.

Malaya prevented Redz's hug by pushing him back and extending her hand.

"Yeah, you know I don't hug anybody."

"Shit, you're hugging Mike's sucker ass."

"That's a different story and you don't have nothing to do with that." Malaya cut her eyes at Damu as he watched her and Redz intensely. She could only hope and pray Damu did not take what Redz said the wrong way.

"Well, Redz, let me get going. It was nice seeing you."

"Not as nice as it was seeing you," Redz said, grabbing his crotch. "Don't forget, me or Mike will come by to holla at you about the business."

"Aight, Redz," Malaya said as she walked away with Damu.

"Look, sis. Go ahead and go home. I got a few things to take care of."

"Okay, bruh. I'll see you later. Are you coming over tonight?"

"I'm not sure right now but tell Anya I'll be calling her."

"Aight, peace, bruh." Malaya jumped into her car and pulled off, wondering how Damu took the encounter with Redz. She knew it had to affect him to some degree, but she wasn't sure how much. Malaya was intrigued when she saw Damu walk by his car like he didn't even own it. *I wonder what he's up to.* Malaya thought.

Jibril Williams

CHAPTER 35

THE PROPOSITION

Velli's mind as well as his heart was in utter turmoil. He couldn't believe Malaya had been lying to him all this time. "How the fuck could I have been so fucking stupid?" Velli paced back and forth in his cell. He hadn't been able to sleep in two days, trying to make sense of the pictures he received in the mail from an anonymous source. "I asked her was she fucking this dude and she swore up and down she wasn't fucking him. Come to find out, this was the same Mike she was dealing with in college," Velli said to himself. The knock at his cell door caused him to spin around with his fists clenched.

"What!"

"Are you, Mr. Williams?" the young C.O. asked.

"Yeah."

"You have a visit, sir. Let me know when you are ready, so I can let you out to go to visitation."

"Yeah, whatever." Velli brushed the new young female officer off, grabbed the pictures off the bed, and looked at them one last time before he wanted to see Malaya. Wiping the tears from his face and stuffing the pictures in his shirt pocket, he exited the cell.

As he stepped into the visitation room, Velli's face exuded pure rage. He approached the officer's desk, where two officers were sitting. "Where's my visit?" Velli asked, still scanning the room.

"Let me see, " the officer said, standing up. "Oh, that's him over there sitting by the vending machine." Velli saw a tall, brown-skinned man stand up, dressed in Versace from head to toe. Velli made his way over to him. He was confused until he got close enough to recognize the man.

"Bitch nigga, you got some heart to bring your bitch ass here to see me," Velli said with pure hatred in his vice.

"Hold up, my nigga. I come in peace. As Salaam Alaikum. This is how you say it, right?"

"Man, get the fuck outta here before I kill your bitch ass!"

"Yeah, and get another life sentence, nigga? Sit down and let's talk about business."

"Nigga, you got five minutes before I turn this visitation room out," Velli said as he took a seat. It took everything in him not to break Mike's haw.

"I know you're fucked up, Velli. I respect a nigga like you. I even had a personal relationship with your man, Stone, back in the day. Matter of fact, Stone paid me to handle a deaf bitch for him a few years back. You two are still cool, right?"

"Your time is ticking, nigga. Spit it out," Velli growled, becoming impatient.

"Well, look, my nigga. I'mma give it to you straight, I want Malaya. We have history, a lot of unfinished business."

'You already got her, don't you?" Velli said while pulling the pictures out of his pocket and tossing them to Mike.

"What the fuck?" Mike looked confused, but he hoped Velli didn't catch his reaction.

"Oh, you got the pictures?" Mike tried to play it cool.

"Yeah, I got the pictures. Now what the fuck you want, nigga?"

"I got fifty G's for you to walk away from Malaya and never look back."

"Man, I'm going to dead that treacherous bitch the first chance I get, right along with whoever is with her."

"Look, Velli, why not profit off the bitch and move on."

"Excuse me, Mr. Williams. You have another visitor on his way back to see you," the C.O. interrupted.

"Aight, bet."

"So, what's it going to be, Velli? Fifty G's or nothing? Like you said, I already got the bitch, so this should just sweeten the deal for you."

"Keep the money and keep that bitch. I believe in karma, what goes around, comes around. Remember, every dog has its day, and I will have mine. Now get the fuck out my face!" Velli yelled.

Mike stood up. "Be easy, my nigga, but remember you stole Malaya from me. Isn't that the same karma you're talking about?" Mike smirked and walked away from Velli.

CHAPTER 36

ALWAYS COMES TO LIGHT

Malaya was so excited to be seeing Velli. It had been a few weeks since the last time she saw him. Holding the fort down in Tampa for Mike had been taking up much of her time, but Velli was understanding. Because he knew she was out there making moves to bring him home so they could be together once again. *Damn, what the hell is taking these fool so long to process my paperwork? These people are so slow today. They need to hurry up. I'm craving to taste my baby's lips today.* Just the thought of Velli's lips on hers, brought a tingle in, between her legs.

"Taylor, Campbell, Reed, Williams." The guard called out the name of the visitors that were ready to be escorted back into the visiting room.

"It's about time,'' Malaya said as she got in line at the door to be escorted back to see her husband.

"Okay, ladies. Stay on the right side of the hall," the guards informed the group as they led them through the door down the corridor. As Malaya and the group of ladies were being led down to the visiting room, there was another group being brought back from the visiting room on the opposite side of the hall.

"Oh shit!" Malaya's heart dropped as she saw Mike in the group being escorted from the visiting room in the other line. Not saying a word, Mike just saluted her and kept it moving. Panic set in as she thought, *Mike just came from seeing Velli. Naw. He must have just come from seeing one of his home boys*, Malaya figured.

***

Billy dropped his pants around his ankles as he sat on the toilet and instantly, he began to shit. "Ahhhh! Damn that felt good," he spoke. It must've been those oatmeal pies he'd eaten earlier, the same pies he stole from the Mexican Mafia. "Fuck them bean eaters." Billy was a new recruit for the Aryan Brotherhood. They had him on a mission for the last two weeks, stealing people's shit in the

unit. Just as Billy dropped another load in the toilet, his cell door came open. Several Mexicans rushed in with nine-inch shanks in their hands.

"Give this to the Aryan Brothers for us, puta maricon!" Billy jumped up to defend himself, but his pants were around his ankles. He didn't have a chance as the Mexicans slammed their shanks into his neck and back numerous times, leaving Billy a bloody mess in his cell.

***

Malaya walked in the visiting room, and the look on Velli's face, let her know her world was about to come to an end.

"As Salaam Alaikum, baby." Velli just stared at Malaya like she was crazy.

"I just saw your boyfriend."

Malaya's palms began to sweat. She began to feel lightheaded. Her breath quickened.

"I don't have a boyfriend. I have a husband that's acting foolish, talking about me having a boyfriend."

"I can't tell, Malaya," Velli said, raising his voice.

"What are you talking about, Velli?"

"That's the same nigga you was fucking with when you was in college." Malaya put her head down. She knew she had fucked up.

"I didn't want to tell you, Velli. I didn't want you to be stressed. I wanted you to focus on getting out, baby."

"Do you love him, Malaya?"

"Hell no! Baby, I love you. What are you talking about?"

"Are you fucking that nigga, Malaya? Don't you lie to me!"

"No! I would never willingly fuck him. I would never do that, Velli. I would never betray you like that."

"Then what the fuck is this?" he said, throwing the pictures in her face. Picking the pictures off the floor, Malaya's eyes burned with hot tears.

"How the fuck could this be?" Malaya said out loud. It was clear to Malaya the pictures must have been taken when Keisha drugged her.

"Hold up, baby. I can explain." Malaya placed the pictures on the table next to Velli as she prepared to reveal the twisted tale of Keisha's deceit.

"I don't want to hear it, Malaya."

"No, you listen to me, Velli. I'm entitled to tell you my side of the story."

"I don't give a fuck—"

"Lockdown, lockdown! All inmates report back to your assigned cells!" the office announced over the loudspeaker.

"Aight, this is an emergency lockdown. Let's go, ladies and gentlemen." The officer quickly began ushering the people out of the visiting room.

"Velli, listen to me, baby, I was drugged." Malaya quickly tried to plead her case.

"Malaya, get the fuck away from me and never bring your ass back up here to see me. I can't believe all the shit we've been through, all the shit I did to get you away from that nigga, Mike. Then you turn around and go back and fuck him?" Grabbing the pictures off the table, Velli stood up and looked down on his wife. "I hate you. Now get the fuck out of here." Velli walked away, leaving Malaya there to wallow in her own tears of despair.

CHAPTER 37

STRICTLY BUSINESS

Malaya cried uncontrollably in the prison parking lot. She couldn't believe what just happened between her and Velli. Not in a million years would she have ever thought Velli would talk to her in the manner he did today. "I know how things may look to him from the looks of the pictures, but damn, I'm his wife. He should have given me the benefit of the doubt. After all, I'm going through all this shit because of him. That mutherfucker Mike pulled this shit on me? I've been selling all his drugs for him, and never did I steal a dime from his ass, and he repays me back like that? I'm going to fuck him over good." Malaya said as she started the car to head home.

Reaching the house, Malaya jumped out the car and ran in the house to find Anya in her bedroom talking on the phone. Once Anya laid eyes on her, she knew something was wrong. "Damu, let me call you back." Anya disconnected her call. "Come on, Malaya, talk to me. What wrong, girl?"

"Velli left me. That nigga went up there to the prison and gave Velli some pictures of us laid up together."

"What the fuck? Hold on, Malaya. That doesn't make any sense."

"Who took the pictures of you?"

"Mike did. When Keisha drugged me, he must have taken some pictures of us together."

"So, you are telling me Mike went up to the prison and gave Velli those pictures?"

"Yeah, sis, that's what he did. I saw him leaving the prison after seeing Velli," Malaya continued, wiping tears from her eyes.

"What did Mike say?"

"He didn't say shit. He was leaving as I was coming in. He waved and kept walking,"

"So, what did Velli say?"

"He just cussed my ass out, told me he hated me, and he never wanted to see me again."

"Girl, you got to tell Velli the truth about what happened at Keisha's house."

"I know, Anya. I tried, but the prison went on an emergency lockdown before I got the chance to tell him what really happened. I don't know when I will be able to see Velli again. With an emergency lockdown, I might not see him for weeks or months. What am I going to do? I can't live without my husband."

"Malaya, you are going to keep living just like you have been living."

"I just got to tell my side of the story. I got to tell him about the drugging and the rape. I have to tell him everything, Anya." A knock at the door interrupted them.

"Who is it?" Anya said while walking towards the door.

""It's Mike," replied in a familiar voice.

"I'm going to body his ass," Malaya said, running towards the closet.

Opening the door for Mike and Redz, Anya's mouth fell wide open.

"What's up, Anya? You got that paper for me?" Mike said as he and Redz stepped inside the house.

"You grimy motherfucker!" Malaya yelled, coming out of the bedroom, cocking Anya's chrome 45. Instinctively, Redz drew his gun, stopping Malaya in her tracks.

"Hold up!" Mike said, putting his hands up in the air. "What the fuck is going on, Malaya?"

"You faggot ass nigga! You gave my husband those pictures of me and you!" Malaya screamed as tears rolled down her face.

"Lay-Lay, put the gun down so we can talk this thing out."

"Yeah, bitch! Put the burner down before I flatline your ass in here." Redz put a firmer grip on his gun.

"Move, Anya!" Malaya screamed.

Anya turned around, stepping closer to Malaya and whispered, "No, girl. Not like that. It can't go down like this. This is my ending, not yours. Give me the gun. I can take care of this. Listen to me, Malaya. Give me the gun." Malaya's hands were still shaking as she held the gun.

"Lay-Lay, I did not give Velli those pictures. He had them when I got there today. He was there waiting for you when I got there. I just showed up to the prison before you did. I went to see Velli to see if I could persuade him to leave you, so we can finish where we left off. I even offered that nigga fifty G's, but he wouldn't accept it. That nigga was on some pride shit and told me to keep the money and you. He was already convinced by the pictures that you were already mine. So, please put the gun down so we can talk. Redz, put your gun away," Mike commanded.

"What? Nigga, you crazy." Redz shook his head.

"Put it away now!" Redz did as he was told.

"Now give Anya the gun, Malaya." Malaya refused to give Anya the gun. She just lowered the gun to her side.

"I don't know how Velli got these pictures, Lay-Lay. I swear, it wasn't from me. They must have come from Keisha."

"Now, how is Keisha going to send them pictures when she is in a coma?"

"Naw, Keisha isn't in a coma anymore. She has been out of her coma for a while now."

This was news to Malaya and Anya. They had been so caught up in the streets, they forgot about Keisha. They could see she was still on her bullshit, right where she left off. Getting her ass beat to the point of near death, still hadn't humbled her.

"Well, tell me this, Mike. Why would you go see my husband and confront him with that bullshit, when he did nothing to hurt you?"

"You don't get it, Lay-Lay. You will always be mine. I will do anything to keep you. I want to bring you off the streets, but I know you won't as long as you believe there's hope for you and Velli to be together. I went to the prison to see if I could convince Velli to walk away from you. I tried to offer him money to do it, something I know most niggas won't refuse."

"What! That's flattering, but I don't fucking want you. We will never be together. I stopped loving you when I saw you kill that girl." Malaya allowed that to slip out her mouth.

What? What are you talking about, Lay-Lay?" Mike took a step closer to Malaya.

I'm talking about the same night I left. I saw you shoot the girl. I was looking through the window. That's what made me leave you." Mike looked shocked. Now it all made sense to him.

"Lay-Lay, you have to understand it wasn't personal, it was all business."

"Whatever, Mike. Just know there will never be another *us* again. Everything between us from now on is just business and nothing personal. Anya, get this nigga his money, so he can get the fuck out this house." The whole time while Mike was waiting for Anya to bring back the money, Malaya just stared at him, clutching Anya's 45.

CHAPTER 38

HISTORY REVEALED

"Here, Malaya. Drink this, it will help you calm your nerves," Anya said, handing her a cup a green tea.

"Thanks, sis."

"Malaya, I don't mean to take you down memory lane after all the stuff that just happened today, but can you tell me what happened the night you left Mike all those years ago?"

"Why do you want to know about that, Anya?" Malaya looked at her friend, confused.

"I want to know everything about Mike before I kill him. Please start with the night you left him."

"Anya, I don't want to talk about that," Malaya said, frowning and taking another dip of her tea.

"Please, Malaya. Tell me," Anya begged.

"Well-well… it was raining that night. Me and Mike had been fussing and fighting for a few days. I was three months pregnant at the time, and he wanted to have sex with me. He was so rough when I was pregnant, he made it so uncomfortable for me to have sex with him. Plus, at that time, I was hearing shit like he was fucking other bitches. So, I refused to have sex with him, because I didn't want to put my baby at risk of getting an STD. I got tired of fighting with him. I was so stressed out. I had my midterm exams coming up in a few days, so I ducked mike's ass for two days to get some rest and study for exams.

"I stayed with one of my friends that I was in school with, but she sold me out to Mike for a few dollars, telling him where I was. He came to her house and forced me to go home with him. I had never seen Mike like that before in my life, his whole demeanor was off that night. I was scared, so I left with him. He told me we were going to go get something to eat and go back to his house, but he had to make an important stop first. We pulled up in front of this small white and gray house on Cain Place N.E. in DC. The street

was so quiet, you could hear the rain beat against the car. Mike got out of the car." Malaya took another sip of her tea, then hesitated.

"Please. Go on, Malaya," Anya pushed on.

"He grabbed some roses out the backseat of the car and told me to sit tight, he'd be right back. I just rolled my eyes at him and laid my head back on the headrest. I watched him walk up the walkway to the house and knock on the door. Moments later, I saw this woman's figure in the doorway. I really didn't get a chance to get a good look at her. She quickly stepped out of view, and Mike stepped into the house and closed the door. I sat there for about twenty minutes, and my mind started to wonder.

"I started to think about the bitches Mike was fucking. I thought he might be fucking one of his bitches right then while I was sitting my dumb ass in the car. I'd had enough. I jumped out the car and ran up to the house I saw Mike go into. I was about to bang on the door, but I heard a crash. I went to the living room window. I-I saw a naked woman in a chair tied up. I just knew I had caught Mike's ass red-handed. I thought I had caught him with another woman, until I saw him walk over to the naked woman and point his gun to her head and blow her brains out.

"I jumped off the porch and I ran. I ran several blocks, until I fell and passed out-right in front of Minnesota Avenue subway station. I woke up in a puddle of blood. I lost my baby right there on the concrete in front of that subway station. Alone."

"So, you never really had an abortion?"

"No, I never had an abortion. I told people that so I wouldn't have to tell them about that night."

"So, did you ever find out who the girl was, Malaya?"

"Yeah, I found out from the news. I saw it on the news the next day and it was in *The Washington Post*. I still have that newspaper clipping."

"What! From all those years ago?"

"I kept it as a constant reminder of what kind of monster Mike really was. It helped me feel like I was making the right decisions by running away from him."

"What was the girl's name?"

"According to the newspaper article, her name was Crystal Williams. The craziest part I don't understand is, why would Mike kill a deaf girl? She couldn't have been much of a threat to him."

"This can't be." Anya looked at Malaya like she was losing her mind. "Malaya, please let me see that news article. Where is it?

"It's inside my old Coach bag in the bedroom closet, where I keep all my important documents." Anya jumped up and ran to the bedroom closet.

"Anya, what's going on?" Malaya asked, following curiously behind her.

"I'll let you know when I see the article." Anya pulled the Coach bag out of the closet and dumped the contents from it onto the bed. "Where is it?" Malaya grabbed a manila envelope, opened it and pulled out an old faded newspaper clipping.

She handed the article to Anya. As she read the heading of the article, it brought tears to her eyes. "DEAF WOMAN FOUND SLAIN IN HER HOME." In the top right-hand corner was a picture of a woman that could have easily been mistaken for Anya or her twin sister.

"Oh shit, Malaya! That was Damu's wife!"

Jibril Williams

CHAPTER 39

PROVEN INNOCENCE

Velli's body dripped with sweat from his intense workout, Beanie Sigel's song, "What Your Life Like," banged in his ears from his mp3 player. As Velli pushed his body to the limit while doing his push-ups, he thought about the pictures he received in the mail. The pure hate he had for Mike made him push harder. Breathing through his nose, he pushed even harder. He just couldn't get the thought out of his mind of how Malaya betrayed him right to his face without hesitation. Getting up from doing his last set of push-ups, Velli paced back and forth in his small cell, while listening to Beanie Sigel tell his story of imprisonment.

Velli hadn't seen or talked to Malaya since the prison went on lockdown twenty-one days ago. To make matters worse, Muhammad moved out the cell. When he came back off his last visit with Malaya, Muhammad was gone. Velli wasn't trippin, he needed the alone time. He had too much shit on his mind to be worried about why his friend moved. Velli wasn't stupid. He knew that it had something to do with Muhammad's daughter getting killed at Malaya's house.

Velli turned around to see the C.O. standing at his cell door staring at him. Velli snatched the ear buds out of his ears.

What?" Velli barked at the C.O.

"Get cleaned up, Mr. Williams. You have a legal visit."

"Give me about fifteen minutes then, I'll be ready."

"Okay," the C.O. said as he walked away from the cell door.

Velli took a quick wash-up, brushed his teeth and slid on a fresh pair of brown khaki pants and shirt, with his black kufi and all-white Air Force Ones. Velli was ready to see his lawyer. He hoped the lawyer had some good news for him. He could really use some. The situation with Malaya really had him in a slump. "It must be some type of good news," Velli said to himself. "Why would the lawyer fly from DC to Florida just to deliver me some bullshit? Unless he is going to play on me for some more money."

The C.O. came back twenty minutes later. "Are you ready, Mr. Williams?" the C.O. called from the other side of the door.

"Yeah, I'm ready," Velli said, grabbing his legal pad off his bunk.

"Mr. Williams, since the prison is on lockdown status, we are going to cuff you and escort you to your legal visit."

Velli hated the fact he would have to see his lawyer for the first time handcuffed like an animal, but what choice did he have? The C.O. opened the tray slot on the cell door, and Velli pushed his hands through it to be cuffed. The tray slot was really meant for the officers to feed the inmates in their cells, without opening the door during lockdown times, but C.O.s also used the tray slot to handcuff the inmates without the risk of getting hurt.

Upon reaching the visiting room, Velli could see that his lawyer was waiting for him in legal room number 3. Velli could see that his lawyer wawa looking over some paperwork. After seeing Velli and the two C.O.s approaching the door, Mr. McCullough stood up and adjusted his tie.

"Hello. Mr. Williams. I'm Mr. McCullough. It's a pleasure to finally meet you." Mr. McCullough extended his hand to Velli, who accepted it with a firm grip.

"Excuse me, Officer. Could you please remove the handcuffs from my client?"

"I don't think that I can do that," the tall C.O. replied.

"Why not?"

"The prison is on lockdown for a murder," the guard said with frustration in his voice.

"Well, did Mr. Williams commit this murder you are talking about?"

"Well... no, sir."

"Okay, so is my client in any way, part of the murder investigation?"

"No, sir."

"Well then, uncuff him, he's not a threat to me or this situation. I would like for my client to be as comfortable as possible. He will

be here with me for the next few hours." That guard uncuffed Velli and walked out of the legal room.

"Fucking flashlight cop," Mr. McCullough said with disdain in his vice. Velli just looked on with a smirk on his face. "How are things going for you, Mr. Williams?"

"Man, just call me Velli. I'm maintaining, just trying to remain strong as a bull in the midst of the storm."

"I feel you, Velli. I feel you." Mr. McCullough was one of those old school lawyers. The ones that grew up around hustlers and pimps, but he was smart enough to watch the game from the side-lines and take his ass to college.

"Well, Velli, I have some very important news for you, and that's why I just sat there calm, cool and collected. Velli, I'm afraid the unprocessed evidence does not link you to the crime scene." Velli sat straight up in his chair.

"What?"

"Hold up, Velli, let me finish. The boot prints recovered from the crime scene do not match the boots you had on the night the police arrested you, nor does the fingerprints found at the crime scene match you either. They have nothing to link you to the crime. Now, I have already filed two motions on your behalf. The first one is a motion under <u>Brady vs. United States.</u> This is a motion saying the government withheld evidence that was in your favor. This is a guaranteed release if the government rules in your favor on this.

"The second motion is a 22.234, which is a motion to the courts of Actual Innocence Claim. I also spoke to the judge about these matters. They state the government has sixty days to contest the new finding in a court hearing. If the government doesn't respond within sixty days, then they will issue an order of immediate release. Now Velli, do you have any questions, so far?" Velli just smiled.

"Damn. Shit is that serious, huh?" Mr. McCullough replied, stroking his salt and pepper beard.

"Will I have to be at the hearing?"

"Not at this time, but if we have a hearing in sixty days after the first hearing, we will set a court date if there's any issues with the new evidence. But for real, Velli, the government can't get around

this new evidence. Your prison days are coming to an end." Hearing this made Velli smile.

"Mr. McCullough, let me ask you something. Do you know whose fingerprints were found at the crime scene?"

"As of right now, I don't know whose fingerprints they are. I can have the prints run through the criminal database, but this is going to cost you because I'm going to have to grease some palms to have this done. So, this will be off the record."

"Yeah, I want the prints run, but I don't want the police to know who the prints belong to."

"Well, Velli, they are probably going to run the prints anyway, so I'll try to find out whose prints they are before the police do."

"I need one more thing from you, McCullough."

"What's that?"

"I need for you not to tell anyone that I'm on my way out, not even my wife."

"Not even your wife? She'll be delighted to know you are on your way home."

"I just want to surprise her, and I don't want to get her all worked up, just in case nothing good comes out of this right away. You know how it is when dealing with the courts."

"Okay, Velli, I can do that."

"Good. I need these last sixty days to think and clear my head," Velli said with murder on his mind.

CHAPTER 40

ANNIHILATION

Redz pulled up in front of Robert Projects. Redz just sat there in his car for a minute, just watching the scene and eyeing a new ass he'd never seen around the projects before. The young lady was wearing the hell out of the Miami Heat jersey and black booty shorts. The streetlights gave just enough light for Redz to see the bottom of her ass cheeks peeking out from under her booty shorts.

Watching the girl walking into the projects, he tried to get at her. Redz was so caught up on the voluptuousness of the girl's ass, he never paid attention to the crack head leaning against the black gate, watching him.

"Yo, my man." The crackhead came off the gate he was leaning on. "Do you got them fifty-dollar pieces? What about them hundred-dollar pieces?" the crackhead asked as he grabbed Redz by the shoulder and spun him around.

"Man what..." Redz was cut off by the crackhead's gun that was now in his face.

"I finally got yo' bitch ass," the crackhead said as he reached in Redz's waistline and removed his gun. Just then a black van pulled up. "Now get your faggot ass in the van before I kill your bitch ass right here, and if you think you are faster than one of these bullets in my gun, then just try me." Redz had no choice but to do what the gunman told him. Redz got into the van and instantly, his lights were out from the blow to the back of his head.

The cold water jolted Redz awake. He could barely move, because he was butt naked and tied to the chair. Once his eyes came into focus, he could see he was in some type of old warehouse. The stink from the place almost made him spill his guts on the floor. He couldn't see anyone, but he could feel the presence of someone standing behind him. The memory of the crackhead outside Robert Projects with the gun came to him. Redz thought this was all about some crackhead wanting some money.

"I got money, if that's what you want." Redz tried to turn his head around to see who was standing behind him. Not getting an answer, Redz kept on talking. "I got two hundred thousand at my house. I can give you the address, and my key to the house. You can go get the money. Just let me go."

Little did Redz know, his kidnapper already knew where he lived, along with his girlfriend and his mother. His kidnapper had been on Redz's line ever since that day at the barbershop. His kidnapper knew Redz was desperate to try to get himself out of the situation, by trying to convince him to go retrieve the money from his house.

"Nigga, I'm not here about no fucking money," Damu whispered in Redz's ear. Redz jumped when he heard his kidnapper's voice.

"Man, please don't hurt me! I was just trying to eat out there in St. Pete."

"Naw, nigga, this ain't about no St. Pete. This is about a debt you owe." This left Redz confused.

"Man, I don't owe nobody shit. I pay all my debts!" Redz cried from his chair.

"Yeah, you do," Anya said as she walked around in front of Redz holding a stun gun. Redz's eyes popped out of his head. Seeing Anya, he knew she knew it was him who raped her and killed her baby. He started to cry out loud, "Please-please, Anya. I'm so sorry."

"You like killing little girls? You like raping women, huh?" Anya's tears began to roll down her face.

"Naw, Anya, that shit with your daughter was an accident. That shit was never supposed to happen."

"But it did happen. You raped me in front of my daughter and you killed my only child in front of me." Redz started to panic once he saw Anya pulling the bone knife out of her pocket.

"Listen to me, Anya." Redz was struggling to get free. "Why you got me tied up in this chair? It was your girl, Keisha, who sent me to Malaya's house. She thought Mike was stashing money at

Malaya's house. She was the one that gave me the key to get in the house. Come on, Anya. Don't do this, please." Another figure stepped from behind Redz with a hatchet in his hand. Redz swallowed hard, recognizing Damu's face from the barbershop. Damu looked at Anya.

"Baby, are you sure you're ready for this?"

"I've never been so sure of anything in my life. I have to do this."

"Then let's get to work." Anya walked over to Redz and placed the stun gun to his neck, sending twenty-five thousand volts through his body, knocking him out cold.

Jibril Williams

CHAPTER 41

TREACHEROUS DECEIT

Ever since Velli told Malaya he was done with her, she focused on making money. Her plan was to make another two hundred thousand dollar drop, give Velli's lawyer another hundred thousand to cover his balance, and leave town to start over with a new life, just her and Anya. She was still madly in love with Velli, but there was no way to convince Velli she didn't betray him. "Damn, I can't believe I lost my husband like this," Malaya thought. "I know one thing, though, Mike is going to get his. He can rest assured of that."

Malaya loaded 3 bricks in her bag and left the house. She was on her way to see Gold Mouth. He'd never placed an order that large before. He always bought 1 or 1 1/2 bricks, but lately, he'd been trying to get Malaya to front him some work without Mike's consent, but Malaya was against it.

Something about Gold Mouth had been different lately. His mannerisms, body language, and his behavior had all been odd and uncharacteristic of the Gold Mouth that Malaya had come to know so well. Malaya reflected back to when Velli was home. He used to always tell Malaya to watch people's body language. The language of the body never lies. He used to stress that so sometimes reading body language could save your life. Malaya had never forgotten those lessons.

Pulling up on Nebraska Avenue, Malaya scanned the block for Gold Mouth. After not seeing him, she pulled over in front of Sharon's corner store. Looking around, she still didn't see Gold Mouth. "Shit," Malaya cussed to herself as she saw a police car slowly riding up the avenue. She knew she couldn't just sit there, so she pulled off to circle the block and called Gold Mouth to see what's holding him up. She hit Gold Mouth's number on speed dial. He answered on the first ring.

"Yeah, Malaya. Where you at?"

"Nigga, where the fuck you at? You got me out here riding around with all this shit in the car and you're nowhere to be found."

"I'm inside the store. I'm on my way out."

"I'm pulling around the front of the store now," Malaya said, disconnecting the call. Pulling back up in front of the store, Gold Mouth was out there, but the scene seemed different. Everyone seemed to be watching her and Gold Mouth. What really caught Malaya's attention was that Gold Mouth was empty handed. No brown paper bag, no bookbag - nothing. Gold Mouth walked up to the passenger side of the car and tried to open the door.

"Unlock the door, baby girl," Gold Mouth said through the window. Malaya waved him around the driver's side of the car. Gold Mouth looked confused. Malaya always let him in the car when he bought work from her. Making his way around to the driver's side, Malaya watched him like a hawk.

"What's good, Malaya? Why you ain't letting me in the car?"

"I'm by myself tonight, so we are going to do this a little different. Give me the money first. I'm going to spin the block and come back with the work."

"Hell no! What part of the game is that? I'm not letting you out of my sight with my money."

Velli always thought Malaya that all money wasn't good money. "Well I'm sorry, we can't do business tonight. You have to catch up with me another time," Malaya said, putting the car in drive.

"Hold up," Gold Mouth said, looking around like something was going to happen. Gold Mouth reached in his waist and pulled his gun and pushed it into Malaya's jawbone. "Bitch, where that shit?" Malaya's heart dropped.

"It's on the floor in the back of the car."

Gold Mouth peeked in the back of the car, and saw the bag on the floor. "Reach back there and grab that bag for me and don't do anything stupid." Malaya had to think fast to get herself out of this situation. Reaching behind the passenger seat, Malaya grabbed the bag with the work in it. As she turned to give Gold Mouth the bag, she yelled out, "There's 5-0!" Gold Mouth quickly looked over his shoulder to see if the police was coming. That is all the time Malaya

needed as she whipped the wheel to the left and smashed hard on the gas, instantly zipping away from Gold Mouth. When Gold Mouth realized that the police weren't behind him, he knew that he just put himself in harm's way with Mike.

Jibril Williams

CHAPTER 42

TAKE IT TO THE GRAVE

Anya scrubbed her body, viciously trying to get the stench of the warehouse out of her hair and off her skin. She knew that she crossed some lines that truly took her outside of the folds of Islam, but she hoped that if Allah was as merciful as she believes he was, then hopefully he'd forgive her for the deeds she committed. Turning the shower off, and wrapping the cheap motel towel around her body, Anya made her way into the room where Damu was sitting in the dark. He was naked in a chair by the window, smoking kush and watching the traffic come and go from the motel.

The light that's coming from outside of the motel outlined Damu's body. Anya loved Damu's body - his whole 6'3" frame was hypnotizing her. The way that he carried himself demonstrated that Damu was a man of high caliber. The way that his hair was cut in a Caesar cut made him the most handsome man that Anya had ever laid eyes on. What they've done tonight only made their bond stronger. Anya walked over to Damu, and straddled his lap. Taking the kush from him, Anya took two long pulls from the weed. "You all right, Damu?" Anya let the smoke ease from her nose.

"Yeah, baby. I'm straight. What about yourself?"

"I'll pull through. I can't say that I'm proud of myself, but if I had to do what I did tonight every day of my life to bring my daughter back, I would."

"I understand, babe. I really do," Damu said while sliding his hand up the back of her towel and stroking her ass cheeks.

"You know we can't ever tell nobody what we did tonight. Not velli, not even Malaya. What we did tonight goes to the grave with us. Promise me that it stays between us, babe." Anya passed the weed back to him.

"I promise, Damu. Our secret will go to the grave with me." Looking into Damu's eyes, Anya began to cry. "Damn, baby, I have

something to tell you. I never wanted to be one who gives you bad news, but I can't keep this from you any longer."

"What's wrong, Anya? Tell me what's on your mind, babe."

Anya put her head down. "I - I know who killed your wife, Crystal." Damu stopped breathing for a minute.

"Come on, babe, let's not play these games. What do you mean, you know who killed my wife?"

"Damu, I'm not playing. I know who killed Crystal."

"Then tell me who the fuck killed my wife." Damu launched in a fit of rage, pushing Anya off his lap.

"It-it was Mike that killed Crystal."

"Now where the hell did you get that from?"

"It's tru, baby. Malaya was there when he did it. She saw him do it with her own eyes. We just found out recently. I'm sorry, Damu, for keeping this from you. I just didn't know how to tell you."

So many thoughts were running through Damu's head. "How could this be?" Damu thought out loud. The wounds of losing his wife were reopening - they were instantly fresh again. "This Earth is not big enough for me and Mike to share. One of us has to go, and I promise you Crystal, that he will be leaving this world long before me..."

CHAPTER 43

CRYSTAL'S STORY TOLD

Malaya hadn't been out the house in two whole days, ever since that nigga, Gold Mouth, tried to rob her. Niggas been blowing her phone up, trying to get work from her, but she had been sending all calls straight to voicemail. She called Mike and informed him that his man, Gold Mouth, tried some foul shit with her. Mike told her to sit tight until he could locate Redz to come through and straighten shit out with Gold Mouth. He couldn't leave St. Pete at the time to personally handle the situation with Gold Mouth, but soon as he could find Redz, he'd send him to handle his disloyal friend. That was two days ago.

Redz had been M.I.A. Mike had been calling every few hours asking Malaya if Redz had come through to holla at her. Mike had left a few voicemails, telling Redz to come and holla at Malaya. To make things worse, Malaya hadn't heard from Anya or Damu in two days either. Neither one of them had been answering their phones. Now Malaya sat on her couch, babysitting her 380 handgun that Damu gave her, while waiting for Anya or Damu to call. She'd left them countless messages on the phone to call her, she even texted them, but there was no response from either of them. *Where the hell is Anya?* Malaya thought.

In times of distress, she liked to confide in Velli. He always knew what to say to smooth her over. Malaya missed her husband so much. Trying to keep her mind off the sadness, Malaya turned the TV on to Channel 8 news, and as if on cue, Anya and Damu walked through the front door. Malaya jumped up and ran to the only family she had left and hugged them like it had been years since she saw them last. "I was so worried about you two. Where the hell you two been? I been calling you and leaving text messages." Mentioning the phone, Damu went to check his before remembering he had turned it off two days ago, and never turned it back on.

"I'm sorry, sis. Me and Anya got caught up in something. We was at the hotel for a few days."

"At the hotel?" Malaya rolled her eyes. "You telling me you were at a hotel for the past few days, while a nigga was out here pulling guns on me, and trying to rob me?" Malaya frowned.

"What? What are you talking about?" Anya joined in as fear settled in her eyes.

"That nigga, Gold Mouth, tried to rob me for some work. I called Mike and told him. He was supposed to send Redz to go holla at that nigga, Gold Mouth, but Redz has been missing in action." The mentioning of Mike and Redz's names released an uneasy feeling into the room and Malaya picked up on it. "What's wrong?" Malaya asked.

"I told Damu Mike is the one that killed his wife." Malaya looked at Damu.

"I'm sorry, bro. I didn't know. All those years, I never knew."

"Don't apologize, sis. How could you have known? You'd never met my wife. Just please tell me everything about the night you witnessed my wife's murder."

"Nooo, Damu. Please. I don't want to relive that night. I think you are better off not knowing the gruesome details."

"Please, Malaya. I need to know. Please, sis."

Malaya retold the story of the night she left Mike, and how she saw Damu's wife's execution from the front porch window. Damu listened to every detail.

"Did Mike ever say why he killed my wife, Malaya?"

"Well, he never knew that I knew he killed her until a few weeks ago, but he did say something about it just being business."

"Just business?"

"Yes—" the news answer on the TV interrupted Malaya's response.

"This is Channel 8's breaking news, coming to you live from Plant City. Angelia McClanahan reporting."

"Yes, this is Angelia McClanahan, and we are at the abandoned slaughterhouse in Plant City. There was a body found yesterday of a man from the Tampa area, by the name of Terrence Blade.

The body was found by four teenagers that crawled through a hole in the abandoned warehouse. The kids are really shaken about what they saw. Sources tell me the victim was found naked and tied to a chair with gunshot wounds to the head. Police describe this as the most gruesome scene they have seen in years. My sources tell me that both of the victim's hands were removed from his body. All of the details are not clear at this moment, and police have not yet determined a motive." When pictures of the victim flashed across the screen, Malaya now knew what her friend and brother-in-law had been doing for the last two days.

Jibril Williams

CHAPTER 44

SPECIAL DELIVERY

The man in the green Chrysler scanned the street where the post office was located. He needed someone to go in the post office and mail his packages off for him. He saw a boy with a worn and tattered LeBron James jersey on, walking with a little girl. They both looked like life wasn't treating them too good, and they could use a few dollars to help them through the day. Rolling down the window, the driver of the Chrysler called out. "Hey, lil man, hey lil man with the LeBron jersey on. Let me holla at you for a minute."

The boy couldn't have been no more than twelve years old, and the little girl couldn't have been more than nine. The way that she clung to the boy wearing the jersey, it was obvious he was her protector. The boy looked at the driver of the Chrysler like he was crazy, and he instantly balled his fists up. He knew firsthand there were a lot of creeps in Florida.

"What you want?" the young boy questioned, while keeping his distance from the car.

"Lil man, I was wondering if you wanted to make a quick hundred bucks." The boy contemplated. He really needed that money as he and his sister hadn't eaten all day.

"Man, I'm not getting in that car with you, and I'm not letting my sister get in that car either." The driver was thrown off the boy's statement.

"No, lil man. It's not that type of party. You see that post office over there?"

"Yeah, I see it."

"All I need you to do is take these two packages in there and mail them off for me. They already been weighed and paid for. They just need to be dropped off at the post office."

"And you going to give me a hundred to do that?" The boy really didn't believe the man driving the Chrysler.

"Yep, that's it."

"Okay, give me the money."

"Hold up. You get fifty now and you get the other fifty when you come back and let me know you dropped the packages inside the post office."

"All right, but I'm not leaving my sister here with you."

"Okay, that's cool with me," the driver said as he handed the two small flat-rate boxes to the kid, along with the fifty-dollar bill.

***

Velli had been in good spirits ever since his lawyer came to see him, delivering the good news. Even though it was too early to say he would be gone within the next sixty days, it had not stopped Velli from preparing for that day just in case. Velli had been going through boxes of mail, throwing away old letters and pictures. He was trying to make his load light, so he didn't have to carry too much stuff when it was time for him to get out.

He came across an old "Get Well Soon" card from Keisha, sent a while back when he was sick with the flu. He reflected back to a time when the brotherhood between Dinkles, Muhammad, and himself were so tight. Even their wives shared the same bond.

Damn! Things have changed so much since then," Velli thought. Opening the card, Velli began to read. "As Salaamu Alaikum, Velli. All praises are due to Allah. I hope you get well soon. Your sister in faith, Keisha."

Then it hit him like a ton of bricks. The handwriting in the card was the same as the handwriting on the envelope sent with the pictures of Malaya and Mike. Velli searched his locker and found the envelope with the pictures still in it and compared the handwriting. It was a match. Thinking back to the day when he confronted Malaya about the pictures, Malaya mentioned something about being drugged. Velli looked at the pictures with a more critical eye. He closely scrutinized everything in the background and realized the pictures were taken in Keisha's house. *So why would Mike and Malaya be in bed together at Keisha's house? Also, who the fuck*

took the pictures? Velli struggled to find the answers to those questions.

***

The kid in the jersey finally came out of the post office moments later. The driver of the Chrysler started to get nervous, because the kid seemed to be taking so damn long to come back. "How did everything go?"

"Man, that line was long as hell, but I did it. Now give me my other fifty."

"Okay, here you go, lil man," the driver handed the kid another fifty-dollar bill.

"Thanks, man." The kid's eyes swelled with delight.

"And this is for you, cutie," the driver said, handing the girl a hundred-dollar bill. Before her brother could stop her, she snatched the money out the driver's hands.

"Man, why you give my sister that money? She didn't do nothing for it."

"Yeah, she did. She went with you, didn't she?"

"Yeah, I guess so."

"Listen, lil man, no matter what, you always look out for your sister. It doesn't matter if she is right or wrong." The kid just shook his head up and down. The Chrysler started to pull away from the curb.

"Hey, man!" the kid called to the driver of the Chrysler. "Man, what's your name?"

The driver yelled back, "Damu, lil man, it's *Damu*."

Jibril Williams

CHAPTER 45

ONE DOWN...

Mike cruised across the Howard Franklin Bridge that allowed commuters to travel from St. Pete to Tampa. The news of Redz's body being found in an abandoned pig slaughtering house, had him in a foul mood. He didn't know exactly who was behind his friend's death, but he had a feeling it was Lil L from St. Pete. Mike and Redz had been trying to take over Lil L's city for months now, but they couldn't get a full grip on St. Pete, because the nigga, Lil L was putting up one helluva fight.

It was like he was always one or two steps ahead of Mike. Thinking about Lil L made Mike check his rearview mirror every few minutes, making sure Lil L or one of his henchmen weren't on his tail. He got word from Biggz that Redz's car had been parked in front of the Roberts Projects. That meant Lil L must have grabbed him in front of the projects. *How the fuck could a nigga just come into my hood and grab my man like that, and nobody see shit?* Mike thought. *I wonder did that nigga, Gold Mouth, have something to do with Redz coming up dead. I heard that nigga used to get down in St. Pete back in the day. All of this is starting to make sense. That's why Gold Mouth tried to rob Malaya.*

Mike had been losing money like crazy, the money out of Tampa had really slowed down. Since Gold Mouth pulled that stunt on Malaya, he had to tell Malaya to lay low and not move any work, until he could get somebody down in Tampa to deal with Gold Mouth. Mike parked on Nebraska Avenue, down the street from Sharon's Corner store. There was no sign of Gold Mouth's fuck boy ass.

Someone was running drugs non-stop out of the trap house on the side of the corner store. Mike knew it wasn't his shit being sold out the trap house. He had an arrangement with the niggas out there on the Ave. They could hustle all day on the Ave, as long as they bought and sold his product. Somebody was in violation. Mike hit a few buttons on his dashboard, and a hidden compartment opened

up on the driver's side door, revealing a black 9mm Ruger. Placing the gun on his hip, Mike got out the car, pulled his hat low over his eyes, and made his way down to the corner store.

Mike walked up on one of the hustlers in front of the store.

"Bossman! What's up?" the youngin' said, looking happy to see Mike.

"I don't know, you tell me, Catfish. Where's that nigga, Gold Mouth at?" Mike scanned the Ave.

"Man, you haven't heard yet? That nigga got boxed with eighty grams and a burner about two days ago, and the homie, Redz, got murked! It was all over the news."

"I heard about Redz, but I knew nothing about Gold Mouth. Who's running the spot?"

"Oh, the nigga Gator been holding shit down since the nigga Gold Mouth got locked up."

"All right, go in the trap and tell Gator I'm out here."

"Okay, bossman," Catfish said, making his way to the trap house on the side of the store. Moments later, Gator came out the trap house, followed by Catfish.

"What's good, Mike?" Gator extended his closed fist to give Mike a pound. Mike accepted it.

"Ain't nothing much. Catfish, let me holla at Gator one-on-one for a minute." Catfish just nodded his head and walked into the corner store.

"Gator, talk and walk with me," Mike said, walking back towards his car. "Where that nigga, Gold Mouth at?"

"Gold Mouth in the county jail. He got caught with some grams and a burner."

"Oh yeah?" Mike acted surprised. "Tell me this. Do you know anything about Gold Mouth trying to rob the Muslim girl that be moving the work for me?" Gator stopped dead in his tracks.

"Mike, man… listen. I had nothing to do with that."

"I didn't ask you if you had something to do with that. I asked did you know anything about it."

"Yeah, that nigga Gold Mouth tried to get your people for a couple of them thangs. Gold Mouth thought maybe you was doing

a bid, that's why you been missing in action for so long, and you had the Muslim girl moving the work until you get out."

"Naw, nigga. I wasn't doing no fucking bid. I was in other places trying to make shit happen," Mike said, getting pissed. "Whose shit you selling out the trap? I know it's not mines, because I haven't put anything out."

"It's Blood's work."

"Do you think that you can handle shit around here and keep the money flowing?"

"Yeah, bossman. I can handle it."

"All right, I am going to give you a shot at it. But I better never catch you selling another nigga's shit on my strip. If so, there will be a price to pay. Do you hear me, Gator?"

"Okay, Mike. I can respect that."

"Being as though everything is understood, tomorrow, I'm going to have two bricks brought by here for you. I want twenty-nine a piece. The first time is a front. Everything after that is cash on delivery." That put a smile on Gator's face.

"All right, Mike. I can handle that." Gator extended his hand to seal the deal he just made with Mike.

"Before we go, one more thing," Mike said, scanning the Ave. "The Muslim woman that works for me is off limits when she comes around through here. Whatever happens to her when she comes through here, happens to you. And if that nigga, Gold Mouth gets out anytime soon, let him know I'm going to kill him." Mike stared at Gator for a moment, pulled his hat farther down on his head, and walked off towards his car.

Jibril Williams

CHAPTER 46

ONE TO GO

After Redz's murder, Anya and Damu had been playing each other close, like they were the new Bonnie and Clyde. Anya's pussy tingled as she watched Damu while sitting in his work truck, the sweat glistened all over his body as he operated the lawnmower. Every time he pushed and pulled on the lawnmower, the muscles in his arms and abs would flex. Anya loved to see Damu with his shirt off and covered in sweat. Feeling herself become moist between her thighs, Anya spoke out loud to herself, "Let me stop being nasty."

To get her mind off Damu, Anya started to take in the neighborhood. New Haven, Florida was so much better than the Tampa area she and Malaya lived in. On the street, every house had a nicely cut lawn, with the hedges finely trimmed. If Damu could get a contract out here, cutting the lawns of the people who lived on this street, his lawn service would be doing really well. The owner of the lawn that Damu was cutting was on some pro-black shit, that's why Damu was hired to cut their lawn, in an attempt to support black-run businesses. *The houses on this street must at least be worth a million dollars or better*, Anya thought.

The house where Damu and his helper, Jose, were working at was the prettiest house on the street. "I can see myself living in something like this one day," Anya said to herself while taking in the beauty of the house, with its private cobblestone driveway and four-car garage. Anya could only imagine what types of cars were hidden behind those doors. The home was a three-story, Mediterranean-style home, with so many windows, she lost count. The house looked like a castle, with its cylinder-shaped design.

The lush grass that surrounded the home was the most beautiful shade of green and was cut in a unique checkerboard pattern. The hedges were cut with such precision, it looked like it was cut by a barber. Anya pondered, *what would it take to live in a home like this?*

Anya's thoughts were interrupted when she saw a tall, dark-skinned lady exit the house, wearing skin-tight yoga pants, so tight Anya could see the woman's camel toe formed between her legs. To highlight her yoga pants, she wore a pink sports bra that revealed her flat, picture-perfect stomach.

She stepped off the porch, walking towards Damu with a glass of tea in her hand. Anya could clearly see the woman didn't have on any panties by the way her ass loosely bounced around when she walked. She walked in front of the lawnmower, cutting Damu's path off. Damu's eyes damn near jumped out his head at seeing Kim like this. He'd been cutting her grass for two months now and never had he seen her in such revealing clothes before. She always dressed business-like.

"Hey, Kim," Damu said, while looking over his shoulder back towards his truck, hoping Anya was not watching Kim's charade.

"Hello, Damu." Kim smiled at him, eyeing his rock-hard abs. "I thought maybe you would like something to drink." Kim handed Damu the glass of tea.

"Oh, thanks." Damu accepted the glass, taking big gulps of the tea, trying to hurry up and get Kim away from him. Finishing the tea, Damu handed the glass back to her. "Thank you, Kim. That was good."

"You're welcome. Would you like another glass?"

"No thank you. I'm good, but it would be nice if you can give Jose a glass for me."

"Okay, I sure will," Kim replied, eyeing Damu sexually, before she walked away, making her ass jiggle. Anya watched from the truck. Seeing how the bitch in the pink conducted herself made Anya want to jump out the truck and beat her ass. Anya was no fool. She knew from the woman's body language she wanted to give Damu some pussy. The woman was so into making her ass clap, she never noticed Anya sitting in the truck, mean-mugging her ass.

The first chance I get, I'm going to have a talk with Damu about Miss Pink, Anya thought. to She saw Miss Pink go into the house and come back out with another glass of tea in her hand. Her generosity made Anya clench her fists. Anya couldn't believe that

Damu ordered another round of this bitch's tea. But then, she saw Miss Pink walk over to Jose and hand him the glass. Anya calmed down some.

"Mommy, Mommy!" a little girl called from the porch.

"Yes, Ashley?" Miss Pink called back.

"Can I ride my bike? I promise I won't go fast. Please Mommy?" the little girl pleaded with her mother.

"Go ahead. Make sure you put on your helmet and don't leave off the street."

"Okay, Mommy." The girl ran back in the house to grab her helmet. Seconds later, the girl came running out the house with her helmet already strapped to her head. She ran off the porch and jumped on her bike, parked in the driveway. She looked so cute on her bike with the training wheels. The little girl could be about seven or eight. Seeing the little girl made Anya think about her daughter so much, she put her head back on the headrest of the truck and closed her eyes.

Anya reflected back to the day she gave birth to A'idah, thirteen long hours of labor. The first word her daughter spoke was Da-Da. Anya smiled as the memories came flooding in. She remembered how beautiful A'idah looked on her first day of school and how she didn't even cry when Anya had to leave her there.

The tears eased from under Anya's closed eyelids. Taking in a deep breath, Anya could still smell the scent of her daughter. Even though the man that took her daughter away was no longer upon this earth, the pain of losing her was never going to go away.

"Mommy! Mommy! Mommy! Daddy's home!" The little girl raced up the street into the driveway. Following closely behind her was a smoke-gray Lamborghini. As Anya opened her eyes, she could not believe her eyes as Mike jumped out the Lamborghini, and the little girl ran and jumped into his arms.

"Hey, Daddy!"

"Hey, little mama. How's my favorite little girl?"

"I'm doing good, just outside riding my bike. I missed you, Daddy." The little girl placed a kiss on Mike's cheek.

"I missed you too, baby."

"And I missed you too," Miss Pink joined in as she strolled from the porch. She didn't have on them pink yoga pants anymore. She had changed into something a little more appropriate, a light-blue summer dress.

"Hey, baby," Mike said, putting his daughter down and embracing her mother, while cupping her ass and sticking his tongue down her throat. Just then Damu and Jose walked from the side of the house, getting ready to load the truck up for the next job. Seeing the two men coming from around the side of the house put Mike on defense.

"Who the fuck are they?"

"Oh, that's the lawn guy. He cuts the grass every two weeks," Kim explained with a straight face. "Damu, can you come over here please? This is my husband, Mike." Damu's name sounded familiar to Mike, but he couldn't place where he'd heard the name. Damu stuck his hand out so Mike could shake it.

"Nice to meet you, sir."

"Likewise," Mike said, while shaking Damu's hand and staring straight into his eyes.

"Okay everything is done and cleaned up out back. You can check the work," Damu said, addressing Mike's wife.

"No need for that. Your work is always good. Thank you, Damu."

"You two have a pleasant day," Damu said, walking away. As they were loading the truck up and pulling away from the house, Anya was sure to stay out of sight.

Anya, who didn't want to say too much in front of Jose, whispered in Damu's ear, "That was him, baby, that was Mike." Damu just kept driving.

"I know, baby, I know."

CHAPTER 47

GIFTS

Keisha sat in her room, mad at the world that someone out there took her friend, Redz, away from her. She couldn't believe he was gone. Even though she used Redz to get what she wanted and to do her dirty work, he actually grew on her and over time, she started to love him, in some sick and twisted kind of way. He was the only person who would lay with her at night and stroke her hair, while wiping away the tears from her face. The violent assault on Keisha brought them together and strengthened their bond.

She didn't know if Mike found out about her and Redz's love affair or not, but it didn't make any difference. Mike was going to catch the beef for that in Keisha's book, anyway. Keisha heard her mother call from the other side of Keisha's bedroom door.

"Keisha!"

"Yeah, Ma!" Keisha was getting annoyed with her mother. All she wanted to do was to be left alone and prepare herself for Redz's funeral tomorrow.

"A package just came for you. I think it's from Redz." Hearing this, Keisha jumped off the bed and opened the door.

"Thank you, Ma," was all she said as she closed the door and sat back on her bed. Looking at the flat rate package, Keisha read the return address. Redz's name jumped out at her. Thinking her secret lover sent her a gift before he died, flattered her. She smiled and cried as she began to open the package.

***

The knock on the door interrupted the family prayer. The family came together for Redz's funeral that would take place the following day. Redz's mother sat there holding a picture of Redz, praying and asking God to forgive her son for his sinful ways, and to have a place in heaven for him so when God called her home, she'd be able to see him again.

Redz's mom was startled by the knock at the door. "I got it," one of the women in the prayer group said. which was. The woman was not one of the family members. She was just a nosy neighbor who came over once she saw all the cars starting to pull up at Redz's mother house. Opening the door, she was greeted by the mailman.

"Hello, ma'am. Is there a Ms. Blade here?"

"Yes, there is, but she's kind of busy right now."

"Okay. Here's a package for her. Can you sign for her?"

"Yes, I can." The lady grabbed the clipboard and signed for the package.

"Thank you so much, ma'am."

"You're welcome," the woman said as she closed the door behind her. Looking at the package, her heart started beating rapidly, seeing the package was sent from Redz. She thought this was a sign from God, and she rushed the package to Ms. Blade.

"You have a package, and it came from your son, Redz," the lady said as she entered back into the living room, stopping Ms. Blade in the middle of her prayer. The thought that her deceased son may have sent her a gift before he died, was unbearable. Being the religious woman Ms. Blade was, she took it as some sign from God that her son was trying to tell her something. She walked over to her nosy neighbor, who was standing with the package. Ms. Blade's hands trembled as she reached out for the box. Seeing her son's nickname on the box brought tears to her eyes. Sitting back down with the package on her lap, Ms. Blade just stared at it. "This must be some kind of sign from the Lord, everybody. I get a package from my son the day before I lay him to rest." Ms. Blade wiped her eyes with the sleeves of her shirt.

"Open the box," the nosy neighbor encouraged Ms. Blade. She was hoping it was some money in there so she could borrow some from Ms. Blade. She knew Redz was out there in them streets, getting money. Ms. Blade pulled the tape from the box, and her heart began to race. Getting the tape off the sealed box was a struggle, and it seemed like it took forever. Ms. Blade looked inside and was confused to see the box stuffed with newspaper.

Feeling around in the box, her hand felt something hard. She pulled the object out the box and unwrapped it. Seeing what she held in her hands made her stomach drop. Ms. Blade held a jar with her son's left hand in it, floating in some clear liquid. The hand bore the word "RAPIST" carved into it. Ms. Blade blacked out.

***

Keisha opened her package from Redz, and her heart almost jumped out of her chest when she saw a hand floating in a jar of liquid. She was about to scream and call for her mother, until she saw the tattoo on the hand. She knew it was Redz's hand. But once she saw the carving of the words "CHILD KILLER," on the inside of the hand, she knew exactly who sent the gift. Keisha placed the jar on the nightstand. She knew she had to make a move soon. It was only a matter of time before she was next. Malaya and Anya were playing for keeps, by any means.

Jibril Williams

CHAPTER 48

MAKING PREPARATIONS

"All right. Did you get everything we need to handle our business?" Damu questioned Anya.

"Yes, baby. To put security on us, I drove seven hours to Atlanta to get everything we need to pull this thing off. But answer this. How do you know that money is at Mike's house?"

"I just do, Anya. You have to trust me on this."

"All right, baby. You know I trust you. You should know I do." She eyed Damu intensely. "I got some good news and bad news."

"Okay, give me the good news," Damu said, putting a handful of French fries in his mouth.

"Malaya will be out the way when we make our move on Mike. She will be on a run for Mike. She will be gone to Texas to meet Mango, to bring the work back to Florida. The bad news is that she is going to make the trip by herself, if I'm going to stay here with you to take care of business. But when she gets back, we will have fifty free bricks of coke we will be sitting on."

"Shit! Anya, that might not be so bad, but we'll worry about the drugs when we get them. Do you think Malaya can handle the drive by herself?"

"Yeah, if nothing happens to spook her."

"All right then, let her make that happen and we will worry about Mike."

Damu and Anya had been plotting on Mike for the last month, trying to figure out his weakness and the best time to get him and his money. They needed this score to be big. Damu needed his bruh out of prison bad. His brother didn't deserve to be where he was. He was a good man. Every time Damu saw Mike, he had to compose himself, so he wouldn't let his emotions get the best of him and blow his cover. Soon he would find out why Mike killed his wife and avenge her death in the process.

"Damu! Are you all right?" Anya asked, touching Damu's clenched fist that rested on the restaurant table.

"Yeah, baby, just ready to get this shit over with and put this behind us, so we can live our lives together." Anya smiled at the sound of that.

"When it's all over, let's relocate, Damu. Let's get out of Florida." Damu thought about it for a minute.

"Whatever you want, gangsta girl." Damu smiled at Anya, and she smiled back.

"Listen, Anya. This goes down in two days, so let's put the finishing touches on the plan and tomorrow, we will do a dry run of the plan and test the walkie-talkies."

"Okay, baby. Let's do it. I'm ready."

"Remember to keep a closed lip about this. Malaya doesn't need to know about this."

"I'm like Alicia Keys, your secrets are safe with me." Anya smiled.

"They better be," Damu said, standing up and dropping a ten-dollar-bill on the table for the waitress. "Are you ready, baby?" Anya got up and walked out behind her lover. "Thanks for meeting me for lunch," Damu added, while kissing her on the forehead.

"It was a pleasure." Anya grinded into him, grabbing a handful of his manhood.

"Baby, I have work to do. I have no time for a quickie. I got to get back to the shop," Damu smiled while protesting.

"All right then. I'll see you tonight," Anya whined while poking her lip out.

"Yeah baby, I'll see you tonight."

"And make sure you bring your mean dick game too."

Damu's ringing phone broke his playtime with Anya. "Hello?" For a second, there was a silence, then a familiar voice on the other end.

"I need a forty-five-dollar hammer and a box of nails, it's time to build a new home." Damu's mouth dropped. Anya watched him. She knew the phone call was important by the way Damu's body language had changed.

"Where you at, slim? All right, I'm on my way." Damu turned and walked away, leaving Anya looking confused.

Jibril Williams

CHAPTER 49

MORAL DILEMMA

Anya stood over her daughter's gravesite, thinking about how her daughter would look if she was still alive. She wondered if the next move she made would be worth it. She was tired of people dying. Even if she killed Mike, how would that honor her daughter's death? How would that stop another mother from getting that phone call, saying she has to bury her son or daughter?

Islam didn't teach her that. Islam teaches love, peace and submission to God. Anya knew she was far from her Islamic teaching, she no longer felt like a Muslim. The humbleness that used to be in her heart was no longer there, the fear of Allah had faded away. Anya touched the headstone of her daughter's grave.

"Hey, Mommy!" A'idah's little voice came to her.

"I've been missing you so much. How have you been?"

"I'm fine, Mama. I been playing with the other kids that are here and flying the angels." It made Anya feel good to know that her daughter is among angels.

"Mommy, are you still going to come here with me like you promised the last time?" This caught Anya by surprise.

"Baby, I don't know about that anymore."

"Why not, Mommy?" A'idah asked, sounding sad.

"Because I haven't been living right, and I don't know if my actions here on Earth will allow me to come where you are, baby." Anya closed her eyes.

"The angels told me if you kill yourself, you will never be forgotten. Is that true? Because you was taught Allah is the most merciful?"

"And He is, A'idah. But He set the rules and set the boundaries. I think I'm going to stay here for a minute, A'idah, and try to make things right. But I want you to know I love you. A'idah, please never forget that."

"I won't, Mama," A'idah giggled. "So, do you love Damu, Mama?"

"How do you know about Damu?"

"Sometimes, I can see you and him together, laughing and hugging. You look so happy, Mama."

"Yes, I love Damu. I wish you were here with us, baby."

"Mama, the angels are calling for me. I have to go. I love you, Mama."

Anya smiled. "I love you too, baby." Anya walked away from her daughter's grave in better shape than she was when she arrived.

CHAPTER 50

TRIP TO TEXAS

Malaya had been in a foul mood for the past few weeks. She was missing Velli so much that she couldn't even sleep soundly at night. It didn't help her when she saw Anya and Damu all hugged up like they were high school sweethearts. If Malaya didn't know any better, she would think Anya and Damu had known each other their whole lives, from the way they were carrying on with one another.

Since Velli had made no efforts to contact her or respond to the endless letters she'd written him, pleading for him to hear her out, she didn't put any details in the letters about the drugs Keisha had given her, or the rape. She needed to tell those details in person. But the fact that Velli hadn't contacted her, was a sure sign he did not want anything to do with her. *Once I come back from this Texas run for Mike*, Malaya thought, *I'm going to drop a hundred grand on Velli's lawyer for the legal fees, then I will make my preparations to move on with my life.* Packing her overnight bag, Malaya made sure she had everything she needed for the trip to Texas.

Malaya was bent out of shape that Anya was not going with her to make the trip this time. They always went together. Malaya felt like this was Damu's idea, since he'd caught feelings for Anya. *He must have convinced Anya not to make the trip with me.*

"Malaya!" Anya called out as she walked in the house.

"Yeah!"

"Come on, girl! You have a plane to catch!"

"All right! I'm on my way out!" Malaya grabbed her overnight bag off the bed and walked out her bedroom into the living room.

Anya was dressed in black sweats and a black hoodie with Timberland boots. Malaya looked at her crazy, she hadn't quite gotten used to Anya's new style.

"You look very ladylike tonight," Malaya said to Anya sarcastically.

"Oh this? This ain't nothing. I feel a little thuggish tonight." Anya brushed off Malaya's sarcasm.

"It looks like you're ready for war," Malaya shot back at Anya.

"Let's go, girl, so you won't miss your flight," Anya said, walking out the house with Malaya following behind her. After getting outside, Malaya noticed Anya wasn't driving her car.

"Whose van is this, Anya?" Malaya asked.

"It's a rental. Damu got it for me. He doesn't want me driving my car and selling shit out of it."

"Oh, that makes sense," Malaya said, but in the back of her mind, she wasn't going for it. The drive to the airport was a quiet one. Anya didn't have much to say, her mind was on the task she and Damu set out to do that night.

"Is everything all right, Anya?"

"Yeah, girl. Why you ask?"

"You just seem a little distant, that's all."

"Girl, I got a lot of shit on my mind. I visited A'idah's grave today. And I just been doing a lot of thinking."

"Okay, sis, but you know if you need to talk, I'm here for you."

"Thank you so much, Malaya. It's nice to know I have you in my corner, no matter what." Pulling up in front of the airport, Anya gave Malaya a hug.

"Remember, Malaya. This run is going to be different. Once you land, you are going straight to Mango's, pick the car up and you are hitting the road, coming straight back this way."

"I know, girl. I just wish you were going with me. I'm going to drive as long as I can. Then I will pull over, get a room to get some rest, then I'm back on the road the first chance I get."

"Okay, sis. You be careful."

"I will, Anya." As Malaya was getting out the van, Anya called after her.

"Malaya!" Her best friend turned around and looked at Anya. "I love you. This will be your last run." Before Malaya could reply, Anya pulled off, leaving Malaya at the curb looking confused.

CHAPTER 51

INVASION

Anya scanned the street where Mike and his family lived. The neighborhood seemed so quiet and peaceful. She and Damu sat there for a minute, watching the house. Anya started having second thoughts about what she and Damu were planning to do, but she couldn't bring herself to say anything. Damu was occupied, screwing the silencers on their guns.

"Are you ready, love?" Damu asked, breaking Anya out of her trance.

"Yeah, babe, I'm ready."

"Put your gloves on and slide the stocking cap over your face," Damu said, handing Anya a gun with a silencer on it. Before they got out the van, Mike's door opened and Mike stepped out.

"Oh, shit!" Anya said. Mike's wife came out behind him and wrapped her arms around him and gave Mike a big wet kiss on his lips.

"He's leaving, Damu."

"What are we going to do now?"

"Just hold up and sit tight."

"We got to make our move now, Damu."

"We can't afford to have a shootout with him on this street, and that will happen if he sees us coming. Plus, we need that money. Just sit tight." Mike walked to his truck, disarmed the alarm, got in, and pulled off.

"I got a plan. Grab the flowers and let's go. We got to move quick." Grabbing the roses out the back of the van, Anya and Damu rushed to the front door. Anya knocked and Damu stood on the side of the door, looking cool and scanning the street.

"Who is it?" Kim called out from behind the door while turning on the porch light.

"You have a special delivery, ma'am!" Kim looked out the peephole but couldn't see through the two dozen roses Anya held in front of her face. Kim saw the roses through the peephole, and her

heart swelled, thinking her husband sent her flowers. She rushed to open the door, but she was sadly mistaken when she was met by Anya's gun.

"Step the fuck back into the house, and if you scream, I'm going to kill you and your daughter." Kim was in shock. She couldn't move. Anya pushed her back into the house, knocking her off her feet, where she fell on the floor. Once Anya was in the house, Damu was tight on her heels, closing the door behind them.

"Bitch, get the fuck up! Where the fuck did your husband go?" Damu yelled at Kim, while pulling his gun from his waistband.

Kim was still trying to get her bearing. "He went to St. Pete," she said, struggling to stand up.

"All right, baby girl. Bring me the phone," Damu ordered Anya. "Who else is in the house?" Damu questioned Kim.

"Nobody. Just me and my daughter. She's upstairs asleep."

"Anya, go check on the little girl, and the rest of the house." Anya took off to follow her man's commands. Damu already knew no one else was in the house. He just wanted to see if Kim would lie to him. "Listen to me, Kim. If you want to live, you will do as I say. Anything outside of that, you and your daughter dies." Kim just nodded her head up and down. "We are going to call your husband. Your job is to get him back to his house ASAP. If you don't get him back here, then you will definitely be sorry. Now you get Mike on the phone, tell him that little Ashley is spitting up blood and you need him to come back to the house to take you to the hospital. You got it?"

"I got it," Kim started to cry.

"What's the number, bitch?"

As soon as she gave up the digits, Damu dialed the number and handed Kim the phone, putting it on speaker phone.

***

Mike pulled over at the Exxon to fill his tank up. While standing next to his truck, the night air felt so good. He just got news that Lil L was kidnapped and was being held at a junkyard in St. Pete. *I*

guess that half a mil ticket I placed on Lil L must have paid off. Now I'm going to do that nigga what he did to Redz, Mike thought. The vibration from his phone broke his train of thought. Seeing that it was Kim calling from the house phone, something was wrong.

"Hello? Kim?"

"Baby, you need to come back home."

"What? What's wrong, baby?"

"It's Ashley, she's spitting up blood. I need you to come and take us to the hospital."

"Okay, baby. I'm on my way. I'm up the street at the gas station." Mike hung up the phone and snatched the pump out of his gas tank. He jumped into his truck, and then pulled out of the gas station. Going eighty miles per hour, he pulled up in front of his house. Mike turned the truck off, jumped out, and ran up the walkway. As soon as he opened the door and called Kim's name, he was knocked unconscious.

Jibril Williams

CHAPTER 52

MANGO

Malaya had a smooth flight from Tampa to Dallas, Texas. The only thing that bothered her was the way Anya was acting. She couldn't get Anya's comment out of her head. "This is going to be your last run." *What did she mean by that*? Malaya thought. The airport was packed. Malaya made her way through the airport to the Hertz rental car department. Just like clockwork, her Audi was immediately pulled up to the checkout place. Malaya hopped in her car and pulled off, heading to Mango's Audi shop.

The traffic was heavy coming from the airport, with people driving recklessly trying to get in and out. Some young girl with a car full of kids cut Malaya off, she had to slam on her brakes to avoid hitting her. Something slid from under the driver's seat and hit the back of Malaya's foot. "What the fuck?" Malaya said, looking down to see what hit her foot. Not seeing it at first, Malaya put her hand down by her feet and felt around. She felt something shiny and hard. She grabbed the object and picked it up. "Damn, a switchblade," Malaya said out loud.

She figured the last person who rented the car must have dropped it. She hit the small button on the side of the knife and a sharp six-inch blade popped out of the top of the knife handle. Malaya smiled. "I like this. I think I might hold onto this," she said, admiring the blade. She popped the blade back into the handle and placed the knife in the side pocket of her jeans.

Malaya pulled up to the Audi car lot, and the place looked deserted, but she knew better. After driving around to the service garage, Mango came out and signaled for her to come in. She got out the car and followed Mango into the garage.

"Hello, Malaya," Mango said, eyeing the gap between her legs.

"Hi, Mango."

"I was hoping since you came by yourself this time we can get to know each other, or at least some type of agreement can be made like me and your friend Keisha had. She was very nice to me, if you

know what I mean. I was also very good to her. You know what I'm saying?" Malaya kept her cool.

"No, thank you. I do appreciate it, but I'm not interested in making no type of agreement with you like that." Mango closed the gap between him and Malaya with swiftness. He grabbed Malaya by her neck.

"Nobody turns down Mango's offer. Do you hear me? You think you're too pretty to give Mango some pussy, puta?" Malaya struggled to get free from Mango's grasp.

"Mango, stop!" Malaya yelled.

"Me stop when I finish fucking you!" Mango said, squeezing his hands tighter around Malaya's neck. He pushed his other hand down the front of her jeans. He unbuttoned her jeans and pushed his hands into her panties. Malaya went stiff as his hand palmed her love box.

"See. I knew you would like it," Mango said as he slid his finger into her. Malaya gasped. Remembering she had the switchblade in her side pocket, she relaxed and eased her hand into her pocket. She pulled the knife out, popping the blade out in one motion. Mango never had a chance as Malaya sliced his face open.

"You bitch, bean-eating motherfucker! You were going to rape me?" Mango shrieked in pain, letting Malaya go, and grabbed his face.

Malaya moved in with the blade pointing at Mango. "Please, I'm sorry, Malaya," Mango said, holding his hands in the air. Malaya stepped closer, putting the blade on his throat.

"Now, I came here to do business, not to get raped. Where is the fucking car?"

"Okay. I'm sorry, Malaya. I'm just used to whenever women say no, they really mean yes. "

"No means no, you fat bitch, especially when it comes to me." He backed away from Malaya, but she was still holding the blade in her hand.

"The truck is outside," Mango said, wiping blood from his face, and trying to stop the wound from bleeding. Malaya walked

behind him, keeping an eye on Mango's every move. Walking over to an old blue Suburban, Mango climbed in the truck and locked the door. The keys were in the ignition. "Once again, I apologize, Malaya."

"Just don't try that shit again, or next time, I'll kill you." Starting the truck, Malaya pulled away, and headed back to Tampa, Florida.

Mango watched as the truck pulled out the car lot. He smiled. "I like 'em feisty," Mango said, still holding his wound.

Jibril Williams

CHAPTER 53

BELIEVE IN GHOSTS

A stinging slap woke Mike up. His vision slowly started to focus. "Nigga, wake yo' dumb ass up," the masked man said, while standing over Mike. Mike tried to move, but his hands and legs were bound tight. Mike focused on the man standing over him.

"We're going to play a game. The name of the game is, 'I ask and you tell.' When I ask a question, you tell me what I need to know, and you are closer to staying alive. But, if you lie or tell me some bullshit, then I'm going to inflict pain on you that's going to bring you closer to death. Understand?"

Mike nodded.

"Okay, question one. Where's the money at?"

"Man, what money?" Mike played his hand with no hesitation. *Phuff.* The gunman put a hole in Mike's kneecap. The silencer on the gun made the shot barely heard, but Mike could be heard as he screamed in pain. "Aaahhhhhhhhhh!" Kim laid on the floor tied up and watching in horror.

"Now, let's try this again. Where is the fuckin' money?"

"Man, it-it's in the closet over there, down the hall on the right." Damu gave Anya a head nod to go check the closet out. Moments later, she came back with a large duffle bag. She opened the bag to reveal nothing but stacks of money.

"That's nice, but where's the real money at? I know it's hidden safe somewhere in this bitch."

"Man, that's it! I'm telling you the truth," Mike pleaded from the floor.

"Maybe that's it," Anya replied, just trying to get it over with as soon as possible. She didn't understand why Damu wasn't ready to kill Mike and get out of there.

"Shut up!" Damu yelled at Anya. He walked over and shot Mike in the hand.

"Aaahhhhhh!" Mike let out a terrifying scream.

"The next time I ask you a question and you don't answer correctly, I'm going to drag your daughter down here and put a hole in her head."

The thought of something happening to Ashley made Mike submit. "All right! Just don't hurt my daughter. The money is in the basement, in the wine cellar. Go to the wine rack and pull the middle bottle on the rack, the wine rack will open up."

"Go check it out," Damu demanded.

Anya took off like lightning. "You better hope she finds it on the first try," Damu said to Mike. "Because I'd love to kill your wife if she doesn't find it." Damu grabbed the walkie-talkie out of his pocket. "Baby girl, how we looking down there?"

"Mmmmm, I'm almost there. I'm in the wine cellar now. I see the rack."

"Mike, let me ask you something. Do you believe in ghosts?" Before Mike could answer, Anya's voice came over the walkie-talkie.

"Bingo! Oh, my God! I found it! It's a small room full of money!"

"All right, get your ass back up here." Anya rushed back to the living room, out of breath.

"We found the money. Let's do what we came to do," Anya pleaded with Damu.

"Just a minute," Damu said, changing the walkie-talkie to a different channel. "Yo, slim, are you there?"

"Yeah," a voice responded over the walkie-talkie.

"Come on in. The rat has been trapped."

Damu turned to Mike. "Like I was saying before, do you believe in ghosts?" Anya didn't know what was going on. She just looked at Damu like he was crazy, through her stocking covering her face. Moments later, the front door opened, and footsteps were heard coming down the hall.

"No, I don't believe in ghosts," Mike said from the floor.

"Well, you should," Velli said as he walked into the living room. Mike's eyes got as big as golf balls. Anya's knees became weak. She had to brace herself on the wall.

"Man! All this is about a bitch?" Mike shouted from the floor.

"Naw, nigga! This is bigger than a bitch. This is about family. This is about fucking with a man's wife. That's off limits." Velli stomped down on Mike's wounded hand. He screamed in pain.

"Let's go get that money, baby girl," Damu told Anya. Anya pulled the mask off.

Mike saw Anya's face and flipped. "You fucking bitch! I took care of you and Malaya!" Anya shot off one of Mike's fingers and followed behind Damu.

"I told you I believe in karma, Mike, but you laughed at me," Velli said as he kicked Mike in the face. Mike's wife screamed from the force of the blow to her husband's head. "Who might this be?" Velli walked over to Kim.

"I'm his wife."

"You picked the wrong nigga to marry. Did he tell you he violated my wife? How he killed my brother's deaf wife for no fucking reason? Did he tell you how he offered me fifty grand for my wife, like she was some type of property that could be bought? But you lay here tied up and crying for this piece of shit."

Damu and Anya came back from getting the money. Damu was carrying three Army duffle bags, while Anya was carrying two duffle bags of her own.

"We got the money, bruh," Damu said as he entered the room. "Anya, you've done enough. Go home and wait for me to get there."

"No, baby, I'm not leaving."

"Anya, please go. We are right behind you." Anya grabbed the duffle bags, threw them over her shoulder, kissed Damu, and made her way to the door. "I'm right behind you, baby. I promise."

"Okay, hurry up."

"It's time for the truth to be told. Mike, the deaf woman you killed for my man Stone, was this man's wife." Damu bent over Kim and slit her throat. Blood poured from her like a running faucet. Mike closed his eyes and turned his head away.

"Now a fair exchange is no robbery, is it?" Damu asked with a wicked grin on his face. He wiped the blood from his knife on

Kim's shirt as she laid there bleeding out like a pig. "Now, tell me why Stone had you kill my wife."

"He wanted the city for himself when Velli got knocked for the murder. He paid me to kill you and the girl, but you wasn't at the house when I got there."

Velli knew Stone was foul. His attorney, Mr. McCullough, informed him that it was Stone's fingerprints at the crime scene. Velli pulled out a gold-plated .45, pointed it at Mike's chest and pulled the trigger. *Boom*! *Boom*! *Boom*! Two shots hit Mike in the chest, and the final shot hit him in the cheek.

"Daddy! Daddy!" the little girl yelled from the top of the stairs.

"Shit!" Damu hissed, as he took off after Mike's daughter.

Velli couldn't let Damu kill that little girl. He caught up with his brother. "Damu, let's go. She can't identify us. Let's go!" Damu and Velli went back downstairs, grabbed the rest of the money, and left Mike and his wife dying on the floor.

CHAPTER 54

Six months later, Velli and Malaya stood face-to-face on the beach of Costa Rica. Malaya looked flawless in her cream-colored silk abaya and her matching hijab. Standing next to them was Anya and Damu. Never in a million years would Velli have thought he would be having a double wedding with his brother and his wife's best friend. It was only right the two couples shared this special moment, after all they had been through together.

Anya looked so happy standing next to Damu as he rubbed her pregnant stomach. While in prison, Velli promised Malaya he would give her the wedding she deserved. Now here he was standing on the beach of Costa Rica, remarrying the woman he adored from the crown of her head to the sole of her feet. All of this was made possible because the courts overturned Velli's conviction and ordered an immediate release.

The money they got from Mike's house, was a little over three million dollars, and the shipment Malaya brought back from Texas, put eighty bricks of pure white between them. Velli smiled, just thinking about the future with his family.

"You both may kiss your brides." Velli and Damu tongued their wives down like it was their first time ever kissing them. The guests went wild with cheers. Malaya blushed as she was hugged and kissed by numerous family members there to enjoy their special day. Velli had flown the entire family in to share the moment.

"I love you, baby," Malaya said as she was continually showered with kisses.

"I love you too, beloved." Velli and Damu just stood there, enjoying the people they loved, and relishing in the fact that everyone was happy for them. Then a figure in the crowd stood out, he looked like he didn't belong there. The fat man made his way towards Velli. Velli bumped his elbow into Damu, getting his attention, and nodding towards the approaching man.

"Hola, my amigo!" the fat guy said as he approached them and handed each a black box.

Velli and Damu opened the boxes, and there laid two of the most expensive Rolex watches they'd ever seen. "Sorry to interrupt this fine day, my friends, but we have business to discuss."

"Well, let's talk," Velli said, getting angrier by the minute because the fat motherfucker was interrupting his wedding day.

"My name is Mango. I'm Mike's supplier, or should I say *was* Mike's supplier before you killed him. Mike was bringing me five million a month. You came and stopped my cash flow for whatever reason. But Mango don't just take losses that easy. Now what we can do is this. I can supply you with product and you can get that five million a month back flowing my way. If not, then I can have you and your whole fucking family wiped out right now."

Mango waved his hand around, bringing Velli's attention to the wedding workers, they were all Mango's people. Mango's people all stood around waiting on his command. Velli couldn't put his family in danger.

"Okay. I'll tell you what, Mango. I'll accept your offer, but under two conditions. One, you deliver all the work to us. Two, I need you to double the shipment." Mango thought about it.

"Doubling the shipment means doubling the money," Mango said, looking Velli in his eyes.

"I know exactly what that means," Velli replied without breaking his stare.

"Okay. Deal, amigo." Mango extended his hand to seal the agreement, and he walked away a happy man.

"Velli, is you crazy? How the hell we going to move double the shipment in a month?" Damu questioned in frustration.

"Easy. You're going to lock Tampa down and I'm going back to D.C. to take my city."

***

"Daddy! Daddy!" The cute little girl ran to her daddy's chest as he laid on South Beach, getting some sun. He flinched a little,

still recovering from a broken collarbone. If it wasn't for his bullet-proof vest, he surely would have been dead.

"Yes, baby?"

"Can I have something to drink?"

"You sure can, baby."

"I miss Mommy," the little girl said, making a sad face. Her comment made him pause and reach for his face where the bullet grazed him, and he remembered how he lost his wife.

"I miss Mommy too, Ashley," Mike said as he reached into the cooler and handed his daughter a bottle of apple juice.

To Be Continued...
Loyal to the Soil 2
Coming Soon

Lock Down Publications and Ca$h Presents assisted publishing packages.

BASIC PACKAGE $499
Editing
Cover Design
Formatting

UPGRADED PACKAGE $800
Typing
Editing
Cover Design
Formatting

ADVANCE PACKAGE $1,200
Typing
Editing
Cover Design
Formatting
Copyright registration
Proofreading
Upload book to Amazon

LDP SUPREME PACKAGE $1,500
Typing
Editing
Cover Design
Formatting
Copyright registration
Proofreading
Set up Amazon account
Upload book to Amazon
Advertise on LDP Amazon and Facebook page

***Other services available upon request. Additional charges
may apply
Lock Down Publications
P.O. Box 944
Stockbridge, GA 30281-9998
Phone # 470 303-9761

Submission Guideline

Submit the first three chapters of your completed manuscript to ldpsubmissions@gmail.com, subject line:
Your book's title. The manuscript must be in a .doc file
and sent as an attachment. Document should be in
Times New Roman, double spaced and in size 12 font.
Also, provide your synopsis and full contact information. If sending multiple submissions, they must
each be in a separate email.

Have a story but no way to send it electronically? You
can still submit to LDP/Ca$h Presents. Send in the first
three chapters, written or typed, of your completed
manuscript to:

LDP: Submissions Dept
Po Box 944
Stockbridge, Ga 30281

*DO NOT send original manuscript. Must be a dupli-
cate.*

Provide your synopsis and a cover letter containing
your full contact information.

Thanks for considering LDP and Ca$h Presents.

NEW RELEASES

QUEEN OF THE ZOO by BLACK MIGO
MOB TIES 4 by SAYNOMORE
THE BRICK MAN by KING RIO
KINGZ OF THE GAME by PLAYA RAY
VICIOUS LOYALTY by KINGPEN
STRAIGHT BEAST MODE by DEKARI
COKE KINGS 5 by T.J. EDWARDS
MONEY GAME 2 by SMOOVE DOLLA
LOYAL TO THE SOIL by JIBRIL WILLIAMS

Jibril Williams

Coming Soon from Lock Down Publications/Ca$h Presents

BLOOD OF A BOSS **VI**

SHADOWS OF THE GAME II

TRAP BASTARD II

By **Askari**

LOYAL TO THE GAME **IV**

By **T.J. & Jelissa**

IF TRUE SAVAGE **VIII**

MIDNIGHT CARTEL IV

DOPE BOY MAGIC IV

CITY OF KINGZ III

NIGHTMARE ON SILENT AVE II

By **Chris Green**

BLAST FOR ME **III**

A SAVAGE DOPEBOY III

CUTTHROAT MAFIA III

DUFFLE BAG CARTEL VII

HEARTLESS GOON VI

By **Ghost**

A HUSTLER'S DECEIT III

KILL ZONE II

BAE BELONGS TO ME III

By **Aryanna**

KING OF THE TRAP III

By **T.J. Edwards**

GORILLAZ IN THE BAY V

3X KRAZY III

STRAIGHT BEAST MODE II

De'Kari

KINGPIN KILLAZ IV

Loyal to the Soil

STREET KINGS III

PAID IN BLOOD III

CARTEL KILLAZ IV

DOPE GODS III

Hood Rich

SINS OF A HUSTLA II

ASAD

RICH $AVAGE II

By Troublesome

YAYO V

Bred In The Game 2

S. Allen

CREAM III

By Yolanda Moore

SON OF A DOPE FIEND III

HEAVEN GOT A GHETTO II

By Renta

LOYALTY AIN'T PROMISED III

By Keith Williams

I'M NOTHING WITHOUT HIS LOVE II

SINS OF A THUG II

TO THE THUG I LOVED BEFORE II

By Monet Dragun

QUIET MONEY IV

EXTENDED CLIP III

THUG LIFE IV

By **Trai'Quan**

THE STREETS MADE ME IV

By **Larry D. Wright**

IF YOU CROSS ME ONCE II

By **Anthony Fields**
THE STREETS WILL NEVER CLOSE II
By **K'ajji**
HARD AND RUTHLESS III
THE BILLIONAIRE BENTLEYS II
Von Diesel
KILLA KOUNTY II
By **Khufu**
MONEY GAME III
By **Smoove Dolla**
A GANGSTA'S KARMA II
By **FLAME**
JACK BOYZ VERSUS DOPE BOYZ
A DOPEBOY'S DREAM III
By **Romell Tukes**
MURDA WAS THE CASE II
Elijah R. Freeman
THE STREETS NEVER LET GO II
By **Robert Baptiste**
AN UNFORESEEN LOVE III
By **Meesha**
KING OF THE TRENCHES II
by **GHOST & TRANAY ADAMS**

MONEY MAFIA II
LOYAL TO THE SOIL II
By **Jibril Williams**
QUEEN OF THE ZOO II
By **Black Migo**
THE BRICK MAN II
By King Rio

Loyal to the Soil

VICIOUS LOYALTY II

By Kingpen

Jibril Williams

Loyal to the Soil

PUSH IT TO THE LIMIT

By **Bre' Hayes**

BLOOD OF A BOSS **I, II, III, IV, V**

SHADOWS OF THE GAME

TRAP BASTARD

By **Askari**

THE STREETS BLEED MURDER **I, II & III**

THE HEART OF A GANGSTA I II& III

By **Jerry Jackson**

CUM FOR ME I II III IV V VI VII

An **LDP Erotica Collaboration**

BRIDE OF A HUSTLA **I II & II**

THE FETTI GIRLS **I, II& III**

CORRUPTED BY A GANGSTA I, II III, IV

BLINDED BY HIS LOVE

THE PRICE YOU PAY FOR LOVE I, II ,III

DOPE GIRL MAGIC I II III

By **Destiny Skai**

WHEN A GOOD GIRL GOES BAD

By **Adrienne**

THE COST OF LOYALTY I II III

By Kweli

A GANGSTER'S REVENGE **I II III & IV**

THE BOSS MAN'S DAUGHTERS I II III IV V

A SAVAGE LOVE **I & II**

BAE BELONGS TO ME I II

A HUSTLER'S DECEIT I, II, III

WHAT BAD BITCHES DO I, II, III

SOUL OF A MONSTER I II III

KILL ZONE

Jibril Williams

A DOPE BOY'S QUEEN I II III

By **Aryanna**

A KINGPIN'S AMBITON

A KINGPIN'S AMBITION **II**

I MURDER FOR THE DOUGH

By **Ambitious**

TRUE SAVAGE I II III IV V VI VII

DOPE BOY MAGIC I, II, III

MIDNIGHT CARTEL I II III

CITY OF KINGZ I II

NIGHTMARE ON SILENT AVE

By **Chris Green**

A DOPEBOY'S PRAYER

By **Eddie "Wolf" Lee**

THE KING CARTEL **I, II & III**

By **Frank Gresham**

THESE NIGGAS AIN'T LOYAL **I, II & III**

By **Nikki Tee**

GANGSTA SHYT **I II &III**

By **CATO**

THE ULTIMATE BETRAYAL

By **Phoenix**

BOSS'N UP **I , II & III**

By **Royal Nicole**

I LOVE YOU TO DEATH

By **Destiny J**

I RIDE FOR MY HITTA

I STILL RIDE FOR MY HITTA

By **Misty Holt**

LOVE & CHASIN' PAPER

Loyal to the Soil

By **Qay Crockett**
TO DIE IN VAIN
SINS OF A HUSTLA

By **ASAD**
BROOKLYN HUSTLAZ

By **Boogsy Morina**
BROOKLYN ON LOCK I & II

By **Sonovia**
GANGSTA CITY

By **Teddy Duke**
A DRUG KING AND HIS DIAMOND I & II III
A DOPEMAN'S RICHES
HER MAN, MINE'S TOO I, II
CASH MONEY HO'S
THE WIFEY I USED TO BE I II

By Nicole Goosby
TRAPHOUSE KING **I II & III**
KINGPIN KILLAZ I II III
STREET KINGS I II
PAID IN BLOOD **I II**
CARTEL KILLAZ I II III
DOPE GODS I II

By **Hood Rich**
LIPSTICK KILLAH **I, II, III**
CRIME OF PASSION I II & III
FRIEND OR FOE I II III

By **Mimi**
STEADY MOBBN' **I, II, III**
THE STREETS STAINED MY SOUL I II

By **Marcellus Allen**

Jibril Williams

WHO SHOT YA **I, II, III**

SON OF A DOPE FIEND I II

HEAVEN GOT A GHETTO

Renta

GORILLAZ IN THE BAY **I II III IV**

TEARS OF A GANGSTA I II

3X KRAZY I II

STRAIGHT BEAST MODE

DE'KARI

TRIGGADALE I II III

MURDAROBER WAS THE CASE

Elijah R. Freeman

GOD BLESS THE TRAPPERS I, II, III

THESE SCANDALOUS STREETS I, II, III

FEAR MY GANGSTA I, II, III IV, V

THESE STREETS DON'T LOVE NOBODY I, II

BURY ME A G I, II, III, IV, V

A GANGSTA'S EMPIRE I, II, III, IV

THE DOPEMAN'S BODYGAURD I II

THE REALEST KILLAZ I II III

THE LAST OF THE OGS I II III

Tranay Adams

THE STREETS ARE CALLING

Duquie Wilson

MARRIED TO A BOSS I II III

By Destiny Skai & Chris Green

KINGZ OF THE GAME I II III IV V VI

Playa Ray

SLAUGHTER GANG I II III

RUTHLESS HEART I II III

Loyal to the Soil

By Willie Slaughter

FUK SHYT

By Blakk Diamond

DON'T F#CK WITH MY HEART I II

By Linnea

ADDICTED TO THE DRAMA I II III

IN THE ARM OF HIS BOSS II

By Jamila

YAYO I II III IV

A SHOOTER'S AMBITION I II

BRED IN THE GAME

By S. Allen

TRAP GOD I II III

RICH $AVAGE

By Troublesome

FOREVER GANGSTA

GLOCKS ON SATIN SHEETS I II

By Adrian Dulan

TOE TAGZ I II III

LEVELS TO THIS SHYT I II

By Ah'Million

KINGPIN DREAMS I II III

By Paper Boi Rari

CONFESSIONS OF A GANGSTA I II III IV

By Nicholas Lock

I'M NOTHING WITHOUT HIS LOVE

SINS OF A THUG

TO THE THUG I LOVED BEFORE

By Monet Dragun

CAUGHT UP IN THE LIFE I II III

THE STREETS NEVER LET GO
By Robert Baptiste
NEW TO THE GAME I II III
MONEY, MURDER & MEMORIES I II III
By **Malik D. Rice**
LIFE OF A SAVAGE I II III
A GANGSTA'S QUR'AN I II III
MURDA SEASON I II III
GANGLAND CARTEL I II III
CHI'RAQ GANGSTAS I II III
KILLERS ON ELM STREET I II III
JACK BOYZ N DA BRONX I II III
A DOPEBOY'S DREAM I II
By **Romell Tukes**
LOYALTY AIN'T PROMISED I II
By Keith Williams
QUIET MONEY I II III
THUG LIFE I II III
EXTENDED CLIP I II
By **Trai'Quan**
THE STREETS MADE ME I II III
By **Larry D. Wright**
THE ULTIMATE SACRIFICE I, II, III, IV, V, VI
KHADIFI
IF YOU CROSS ME ONCE
ANGEL I II
IN THE BLINK OF AN EYE
By **Anthony Fields**
THE LIFE OF A HOOD STAR
By Ca$h & Rashia Wilson

Loyal to the Soil

THE STREETS WILL NEVER CLOSE

By K'ajji

CREAM I II

By Yolanda Moore

NIGHTMARES OF A HUSTLA I II III

By King Dream

CONCRETE KILLA I II

VICIOUS LOYALTY

By Kingpen

HARD AND RUTHLESS I II

MOB TOWN 251

THE BILLIONAIRE BENTLEYS

By Von Diesel

GHOST MOB

Stilloan Robinson

MOB TIES I II III IV

By SayNoMore

BODYMORE MURDERLAND I II III

By Delmont Player

FOR THE LOVE OF A BOSS

By C. D. Blue

MOBBED UP I II III IV

THE BRICK MAN

By King Rio

KILLA KOUNTY

By Khufu

MONEY GAME I II

By Smoove Dolla

A GANGSTA'S KARMA

By FLAME

KING OF THE TRENCHES II
by **GHOST & TRANAY ADAMS**
QUEEN OF THE ZOO
By **Black Migo**

BOOKS BY LDP'S CEO, CA$H

TRUST IN NO MAN

TRUST IN NO MAN 2

TRUST IN NO MAN 3

BONDED BY BLOOD

SHORTY GOT A THUG

THUGS CRY

THUGS CRY 2

THUGS CRY 3

TRUST NO BITCH

TRUST NO BITCH 2

TRUST NO BITCH 3

TIL MY CASKET DROPS

RESTRAINING ORDER

RESTRAINING ORDER 2

IN LOVE WITH A CONVICT

LIFE OF A HOOD STAR

Jibril Williams